FROM DESPAIR
TO FORTUNE

From Despair To Fortune

By
Cal Campbell

E-BookTime, LLC
Montgomery, Alabama

From Despair to Fortune

Library of Congress Control Number: 2013940341

ISBN: 978-1-60862-494-2

First Edition
Published May 2013
E-BookTime, LLC
6598 Pumpkin Road
Montgomery, AL 36108
www.e-booktime.com

Dedication

The author would like to dedicate this book to the pioneer settlers of northwest South Dakota, who were instrumental in changing the barren and wind-swept plains into a profitable ranching area.

My grandparents, the Campbells and McCaffrees chose to leave the fairly comfortable life in southern Iowa to take advantage of the Enlarged Homestead Act of 1909. My grandparents gladly accepted the 320 acres given to them by the United States Government.

I lived in Rapid City, South Dakota, until leaving for The University of South Dakota in 1954. My Uncle John and Aunt Floy, who lived on a ranch near Faith, were an inspiration to write this historical novel.

Acknowledgements

I would like to acknowledge the assistance and encouragement given by my loyal wife Betty J. Campbell, whose editing skills I depend upon in writing my books.

The poem in Chapter 1 is reprinted from: *Bedside Book of Bad Boys of the Black Hills* by Barbara Fifer (Farcountry Press, 2008.)

Preface

FROM DESPAIR TO FORTUNE is intended to be an historical novel about two fictional families living in western South Dakota from the mid-1800's until the end of World War II.

The mention of real characters living at the time is genuine and their actions were real. Also, the time line is accurate as much as I can discern. My grandparents moved from southern Iowa to take advantage of the 1909 Homestead Act.

My much older brother and sister were born in this barren part of South Dakota. The hardships endured by the families are to be admired.

I can remember visiting my Uncle John and Aunt Floy's cattle ranch just outside of Faith, South Dakota. Actually, their ranch was closer to Mud Butte. My uncle died in 1952 and my aunt moved to California to live with her sister.

Uncle John and Aunt Floy lived without the modern conveniences that exist today. The tar-paper very modest home in which they lived had none of the modern appliances of present day ranches in the area.

In fact, they had no electricity. They used a two-hole outhouse about fifteen feet from their back door and the water was obtained from a well that my uncle had to pump to bring water to the surface.

Today, the ranchers in this area have indoor plumbing, telephones, television, and all of the other comforts enjoyed by their town-dwelling neighbors.

The differences can also be seen in the type of cattle raised on the plains. Many of the white-faced Herefords have been replaced with registered Black Angus. Ranchers still probably thin their herds for the winter months by shipping the cattle to Chicago and Omaha.

Instead of chasing the lost calves with their trusted "cutting horses" many now use all-wheel terrain vehicles and pick-ups. I will bet that the ranchers still have their favorite riding horses.

It would not be surprising to me that a few of the ranchers have a small plane and marked-off grass runways to reach destinations in a much faster way.

I remember when Highway 212 was nothing but mud and some gravel. Today the route is a paved two-lane highway connecting Minnesota with South Dakota before winding into Wyoming and beyond. Since I have not been to this part of the state for over fifty years, the highway could now be four-lane.

I hope you enjoy reading this book as much as I have enjoyed reminiscing and researching the past.

Chapter 1

The Hall Brothers

James Hall was only 19 years old and his younger brother Frank had just had his 18th birthday. Both young men lived on a small ranch in eastern Wyoming on the border with South Dakota.

The two brothers were similar in looks; however, James was very tall for being only 19 and measured close to 6 feet 5 inches. James also had fair skin and curly red hair. He was very shy and embarrassed by his many freckles.

Frank was somewhat smaller in stature standing only 6 feet 2 inches. Unlike his brother, Frank had dark auburn straight hair and a somewhat darker complexion.

As both their father and mother were tall and the boys' grandparents had been very large for individuals in the mid-1800's, it was not surprising that all of their neighbors considered the Hall family to be very big people.

The family had difficulty in maintaining the ranch as their land was poor. After two summers of drought they barely had enough grass to feed their very small herd of long-horn cattle that they had bought in Cheyenne, Wyoming, from a group of cowboys driving a herd from Texas.

Today, many would say the family had a "cash flow" problem. With only nine cattle in their small herd, there really was no work for the two boys as their father Don could manage the ranch by himself.

The four mouths to feed put the family further and further in debt to the only store in Newcastle, Wyoming. In fact, the owner of the general store had told the Hall family that he could no longer carry their markers, and they needed to settle their back debts in a month. Otherwise, Mr. Larson could no longer give them grocery staples and run a "tab."

It was early in May that the two brothers decided to leave the ranch and seek job opportunities across the border in South Dakota.

The Hall family had only one rifle to keep the coyotes at bay when the new calves were born in the spring. Therefore, the boys started their adventure without horses, a rifle or a pistol. Neither boy had very warm clothes to start the long journey, but their mother, Mary Ann, gave each a thread-bare blanket.

With their well-worn cowboy boots the boys headed east. As their father needed the one "cutting horse" for the ranch, the boys were to walk into South Dakota. Their mother gave James and Frank a few biscuits and a little coffee and sent them on their way. Frank also carried a hunting knife.

The younger son Frank had practiced and was a good shot with his sling-shot. James hoped that his brother could shoot a rabbit and supply them with some meat on their intended long walk.

It was nearing dusk when the Hall brothers sighted a campfire about a half mile ahead. The smell of boiling coffee and fresh meat meant that the campers had food that they might share. The younger brother Frank was the more cautious of the two and hesitated about walking toward the campfire, not knowing if it was safe.

It was at this point that James stated, "Frank, we have absolutely nothing of value except the clothes on our back." Therefore, Frank agreed with his big brother, and they announced their arrival, so as not to upset the two men huddled beside the warm fire.

To the brothers' delight the two men, A.J. Allen and Louis Curry, invited the two boys to share their meal of biscuits and a rabbit they were cooking. The evening was cool, so all four of the men enjoyed the hot coffee boiling on the pine stick fire.

With a full stomach for the first time in days, James and Frank settled down for what they thought would be a peaceful sleep.

The men had hobbled several horses so they would not wander away in the night.

Perhaps after not eating for a day, it was Frank who awoke about midnight to urgently disappear into the pine forest to relieve himself. James had warned Frank not to stuff himself with so many biscuits and rabbit or else risk the "trots."

It was during Frank's absence that a posse of men, led by the local sheriff from Rapid City, woke the three remaining men and immediately arrested them for stealing horses from the Salisbury-Gilmer Stage Company. The stage company was located in Crook City, not far from Rapid City.

Frank hid behind a large bolder, not far from the camp, and witnessed the arrest. As he did not want to risk being the fourth captive, he was very silent, trembling with fear.

The posse took the three men and their horses into Rapid City and locked them in a barn. Immediately, James Hall began to beg the sheriff to release him since he did not know that the horses were stolen and had only arrived at the campsite that evening.

As soon as the three men arrived in Rapid City, the owners of the Stage Company identified the horses as belonging to them. In fact, the owners of the Stage Company were so happy to have their horses returned that they paid for drinks to the waiting group of citizens who had witnessed the posse and men coming into town.

In early evening, Judge Robert Burleigh conducted a hearing and later turned the evidence over to the grand jury to make a decision as to the three men's guilt or innocence.

Perhaps, due to the group of cowboys having free liquor supplied by the owners of the Stage Company, a group of vigilantes, all with masks, broke into the barn where the three men were being held captive and forced them up a near-by hill.

All the way up the hill, the townspeople could hear the young Hall boy crying and begging for his life. However, the vigilantes were too drunk to listen to the pitiful screams and proceeded with a hanging.

By law, the three men were to have been given the standard hanging for horse thieves. This meant that the three would be placed on horses with their hands tied behind them. Then the horses would be slapped on their hindquarters, and after taking off, the men would be left dangling from their ropes with broken necks.

However, when Judge Burleigh made it to the top of the hill the next morning, he assumed the role of coroner and conducted his inquest. He found that the knots had been so poorly formed that the three men had died of asphyxiation – not broken necks as horse thieves were supposed to have died. To be strangled was a slow and very painful death.

All three of the men were taller than the average man in the 1800's, so it was not surprising that all three men had their feet touching the ground. This probably accounted for the strangling and not the broken necks.

In the wild west of the mid-1800's justice was, at times, too quickly carried out – this was one example where a few citizens of Rapid City felt real remorse.

In the meantime, after waiting until the posse had disappeared into the night, Frank carefully took a few of the supplies discarded by Allen and Curry. He was cautious in not taking everything and carefully brushed away his footprints so if the sheriff returned he would find most of what was brought to the camp by the horse thieves.

Frank walked all night to distance himself from Rapid City not knowing what would happen to his older brother. However, he knew what they did with horse thieves.

He hoped for a fair trial and prayed that Allen and Curry would verify James' story of having just arrived that evening. Perhaps, just perhaps, his brother would be released.

About four or five in the morning, Frank spotted a ranch in the distance. He decided to take a chance and stop and ask for directions to the nearest town. If the rancher and his wife were honest, hardworking ranchers like his parents, maybe they would have him stay for breakfast.

Frank dare not tell the ranchers, John and Ellen Swango, what had happened during the night. Rather, he told the couple that he was forced to leave his parents' ranch in Wyoming. Although they loved their boy, they just could not afford to have another mouth to feed. He purposefully did not tell the Swangos of his brother James.

As the Swangos were more prosperous and had a vast herd of the very best cattle, Mr. Swango asked if

Frank would like a job. John and Ellen had a bunk-house for their hired wranglers.

John, together with a few of the men on the ranch, fitted Frank with clothes, a fine horse and saddle. They did not offer Frank a Colt six-shooter as they really did not know anything about this stranger appearing in the very early morning.

After enjoying a big breakfast with the boys who worked for the Swangos, Frank was expected to ride out with the group and look for stray calves that may have been separated from the herd during the night.

It was difficult for Frank to keep from falling asleep in his saddle. Anyway, the chestnut cutting horse that they loaned Frank did most of the work that day and Frank hardly had to touch the reins for the horse they called Snip.

After a week of working on the ranch from sunup until sundown, the cowboys asked Frank if he would like to join them for a night on the town in Rapid City.

Although Frank was at first hesitant, he agreed to join the group. Frank purposely did not tell the Swangos his last name and neither his new employer nor his fellow cowboys asked. In those days, the pay was given in cash. Therefore, last names were not necessary.

While in a Rapid City bar, a local asked the cowboys from the Swango ranch if they would like to hear the story of the hanging of the horse thieves. After the story the local cowboy wanted them to ride up the nearby hill as they had posted a sign that would warn any potential outlaws to think twice about stealing anything from a Rapid City resident.

After a short ride up the rather steep hill the Swango cowboys read the following sign that was posted directly under the "hanging tree."

The sign was printed with the following words:

HORSE THIEVES BEWARE

Here lie the bodies of Allen, Curry and Hall.
Like other thieves, they had their rise, decline and fall;
On yon pine tree they hung till dead,
And here they found a lonely bed.
Then be a little cautious how you gobble horses up,
For every horse you pick up here, adds sorrow to your cup;
We're bound to stop this business, or hang you to a tree,
For we've hemp and hands enough in town to swing the whole damn clan.

Needless to say, Frank hid his sorrow and with tears in his eyes he rode alone back to the ranch. Frank could not sleep and the other cowboys in the bunkhouse heard sobs in the night. They all snickered and thought that the young man was merely homesick for his parents back in Wyoming.

Chapter 2

Revenge

For about a month following his night in Rapid City, all Frank Hall could think about was his older brother swinging from the pine tree overlooking Rapid City. The other wranglers on the ranch noticed that Frank was often lost in thought and appeared "on edge" and moody. Often, he would lose his temper over the most mundane of events.

Frank had made a close friend of Tex Bennett, a drifter like himself, from Texas. Tex had worked for Mr. Swango for several years and was an expert with his Colt .45. He could shoot the burning wick from a candle thirty yards away.

Following what seemed like an eternity, but really only about three months, Frank had saved enough of his wages to buy a used Colt .45 from one of the cowboys on the Swango ranch.

Frank then begged Tex to teach him to shoot and to quick draw from his oiled holster. Tex did not question why Frank wanted to quick draw and to shoot with accuracy. The only targets on the Swango ranch were rattlesnakes and the coyotes.

The coyotes were "taken out" with a rifle and the rattlesnakes were "usually" far enough away that a cowboy could shoot the snake without needing to "quick draw."

No, the only reason to "quick draw" with accuracy was to participate in a gun duel with another man. The attitude that Frank had begun demonstrating started to worry Tex and a few of the other wranglers. Even Mr. Swango had noticed a change in young Frank.

Finally, after persuading Frank to have a few shots of whiskey in the bunkhouse after supper one evening, Frank broke down and told the story of how his older brother James had been hung in Rapid City by a group of drunken vigilantes.

An old Mexican cowboy by the name of Luis Garcia "spilled the beans" on Frank and told Mr. Swango the story of Frank's brother James. Mr. Swango became interested in the story as he too had trouble with Lou Gilmer of the Salisbury-Gilmer Stage Company.

What happened prior to Frank arriving at the Swango ranch was that Mrs. Swango and her daughter Virginia had been stopped on the road to Rapid City by Lou Gilmer and a few of his friends.

Lou stopped the Swango buggy and proceeded to pull the two ladies to the ground and attempted to rape

Mrs. Swango. Lou Gilmer's friends restrained Virginia by whipping her and tearing her clothes.

However, before the group could seriously hurt Virginia, a group of cowboys from the Swango ranch rode to the rescue. After a lengthy gun battle, the Gilmer gang outraced the cowboys back to town. The only casualty to Virginia was a long ugly scar on her very beautiful face. This was caused by Lou Gilmer's whip.

None of the Gilmer gang or the cowboys was killed in the gun fight. However, one of Swango's wranglers had to wear a sling on his arm caused by a bullet to his upper shoulder. This prevented the cowhand from working for nearly a month.

Immediately, Mr. Swango rode into town to report the incident. However, since Lou Gilmer had control of the town, the sheriff dismissed the charges and told Swango to leave town and forget what he "believed" to have happened on the trail.

Now Frank had an ally in the pent-up rage against the Salisbury-Gilmer Stage Company. Frank thought that if Lou Gilmer had not bought all of those free drinks on the night of the hanging that the vigilantes would never have had the nerve to break his brother James out of the barn and proceed with the hanging.

It was a bit unusual that Mr. Swango would invite one of his wranglers to dinner in his fine home with his wife and beautiful daughter Virginia. However, Mr. Swango had developed a plan to extract revenge on Gilmer of the Salisbury-Gilmer Stage Company.

Mr. Swango thought that with a fine dinner of the very best steak and wine he could persuade the young Frank to "take out" the slick Mr. Gilmer. Also, as an upstanding citizen with much to lose if he were implicated in the plot, he wanted Frank to take all of the risks and to distance himself from the assassination attempt on Mr. Gilmer.

The plan was "hatched" that evening. With all the practice on shooting that Frank had received from Tex, the young Hall boy thought he could even the score all by himself.

But Mr. Swango, being older and wiser, thought that they needed more of an edge than a fair gunfight. This is where the old Mexican Luis Garcia came into the picture.

Mr. Swango brought Garcia to the big house, and together they shared a drink on the spacious sprawling porch. (Mr. Swango would never let a Mexican in his home.) Mr. Swango knew that Luis was not of a mind to bushwhack Mr. Gilmer.

Nevertheless, Luis Garcia had begged Mr. Swango to bring his brother Jose from Mexico to work on the ranch. The reason that Mr. Swango had not sent for Jose before was that after many inquiries he found that Jose had been in and out of jail and was somewhat of an unsavory character.

It was also rumored that Jose had run with a group of outlaws terrifying settlers on the Texas border. This time Mr. Swango was all too happy for Garcia to contact his brother and bring him to the ranch. The plan on how to settle the score with Mr. Gilmer was now taking shape.

It was a slow process in the mid-1800's to first contact Jose, and then for the Garcia brother to travel to western South Dakota. In the meantime, Frank polished his gun handling abilities and was gaining both quickness and accuracy with his Colt .45 pistol.

When Jose Garcia finally arrived at the Swango ranch, the other cowboys stayed their distance as Jose was as mean a character as they had ever seen in that part of the country.

Jose had long greasy hair and a long scar that started below his left eye and ran down to just above his unshaven jaw. As Jose had a habit of chewing cigars, his teeth were stained a dirty yellow.

Also, the wranglers on the ranch immediately knew he was a "gunfighter" as he strapped his two pistols low on his belt and had the two holsters tied down with rawhide cords.

The plan was now developing, and both Mr. Swango and Frank wanted the deed completed with due haste. Anyway, the Swangos did not want Jose on their ranch any longer than necessary.

Mr. Swango had watched young Frank practice drawing and shooting and thought that he should not risk the death of this young man when he had hired a true professional to take care of the shooting.

Therefore, Mr. Swango persuaded Frank to practice with a sawed off shotgun that Jose had brought with him from Mexico.

A meeting was held in the Swango barn with John Swango, Jose, Jose's brother Luis and Frank in attendance. Mr. Swango made all the men swear to secrecy about the plan of killing Gilmer. The reason was that although Swango wanted very much to get rid of Gilmer, he did not want to be implicated. With Luis Garcia serving as the interpreter, Jose was given his instructions on just how to draw Gilmer into a gunfight without being arrested.

The plan was to wait until there was a moonless night and then have Jose start an argument in a Rapid City saloon with Lou Gilmer, hoping the two would step into the street for a duel.

In Jose's broken English he asked, "How will I identify this hombre Gilmore?"

As Jose had never seen Mr. Gilmore, it was Luis Garcia who had to describe Gilmore. He stated, "That son-of-a-bitch Gilmore has white wavy hair worn down to his shoulders and has a handle-bar mustache."

In case Jose was not able to "bring down" Gilmer, then Frank would be waiting in the shadows with the sawed-off shotgun ready to finish the job.

The very ugly Jose strode into the bar where they knew Gilmer liked to challenge the other citizens in a high stakes poker game.

Jose motioned to the others that he would like to join in the game. Perhaps Jose understood English better than Frank and Mr. Swango had believed because he understood what the other players at the table were saying. Gilmer was known to have a bad temper and perhaps Jose could entice him into a gunfight.

The dealer by the name of Johnnie broke the seal of a fresh deck of cards and after shuffling the cards passed the deck to his right for a cut. He then dealt the cards clockwise to his left.

The game would be five card draw with no limit on the bets. Jose thought to himself, *It was a good thing that hombre Swango gave me a good bankroll to stay in this lively game.*

Picking up the cards Jose found himself with a pair of jacks. He thought, *I had better make my money last until I get a chance to deal the cards.* So he threw in the cards without making a bet.

It should be known that Jose was no stranger to poker as he would often venture over to El Paso, Texas, for a game. Across the table Gilmer played a shrewd and careful game.

Suddenly Jose found himself holding three nines. He considered them, decided to stay and on the draw picked up a pair of jacks. With this hand he won a small pot. Jose also won the next two hands.

Mr. Gilmore smirked at Jose and stated, "For a Mexican that has not played that much poker you seem to be a lucky hombre." Jose thought to himself, *Just you wait until I get the deal and you will see real luck.*

Jose drew nothing on the following hand and threw in, but on the next he won a fair-sized pot. Jose found himself feeling a little bit regretful as he knew that with his plan the game would never be completed and all the money he could have won would be lost.

When it was Jose's turn to deal, he shuffled and easily built up a bottom stock from selected discards. He passed the cards to his right for a cut, then picked up the deck and shifted the cut in a smoothly done movement and proceeded to deal swiftly. He built his own hand from the bottom until he held the three cards he wanted.

All of the players at the table threw in their hands, except for Gilmore.

Seeing Jose dealing off the bottom of the deck, Gilmer grabbed Jose's wrist and at the same time pulled his Colt .45. A quick thinking bartender pulled his shotgun from under the counter and halted Gilmer from firing.

The bartender told both Jose and Gilmer to step outside to settle their differences. Once outside both men agreed to take ten paces, turn and fire. However, Jose took only nine paces turned and shot the gun from Gilmer's hand. Jose's second shoot struck Gilmer between the eyes.

The sheriff collected several witnesses and they all told the same story that Gilmer had called Jose out and indeed this was a fair fight.

It was now the duty of the Sheriff to tell Jose to get out of town and never to return. After a short ride to the Swango ranch to collect his $1,000 bounty, Jose headed, with due haste, back to Mexico.

Indeed, the revenge that Frank had sought was complete and he was not implicated. Frank also rode out of town without anyone seeing him.

"I hope my mother was right in courting Virginia. What if she already has a steady fellow?" He thought about turning back several times during the long ride.

Frank Hall

Chapter 3

Frank Returns Home

Frank had now spent nearly five years on the Swango ranch and thought that he needed to head back to his parents' home to check on them and tell them the bad news concerning their son James.

As a reward for participating in the ambush and also to distance himself from Frank Hall who might have been suspected of being involved in Gilmer's death, John Swango gave Frank several of his best cattle to take back to Wyoming.

In fact, there were over twenty head of cattle to take back to Wyoming. As there could be cattle rustlers on the trail, Frank persuaded his friend Tex to accompany him back to Wyoming. In this arrangement one could sleep while the other wrangler could keep watch over the cattle.

Needless to say, the parents were very happy to see Frank, but also grieved after hearing that their other son James had died.

In all the years after arriving home, Frank never did tell his parents how James had died. Instead, he told his parents that James had died in a freak accident while he was attempting to break a horse for riding.

Frank's mother asked, "Frank, did you meet any young ladies the past five years you were on the Swango's ranch?"

Frank answered, "Yes, Mom and after I establish myself, and have a nest egg, I will go back to the Swangos and court their daughter Virginia. Hopefully, I will be able to secure the blessings of her parents, and I can begin courting this beautiful blond girl with the cute round face." Purposely he did not tell his parents of Virginia's scar on her otherwise beautiful young face.

Frank's mother had always wanted grandchildren and thought that perhaps their son should not wait too long. In fact, she stated, "You know there may be other fellows who would step in and sweep this cute little filly away from you."

Frank's answer to his mother's urgency was, "Don't worry Mom, Virginia is away at an all-girls boarding school and will not be returning to the ranch for at least two years."

"Well," Frank's mother stated, "there sure ain't no girls in Newcastle that you would want anything to do with as they are all either ugly or come from poor ranch families such as ours."

After returning to his parent's ranch near Newcastle, Wyoming, it was time to brand the large herd of cattle that Mr. Swango had given Frank.

Frank persuaded Tex to stay a few days to assist in this very back-breaking task. As his father Don was aging and had lost a lot of his strength it was either have Tex assist or else attempt to hire another cowhand.

Tex was anxious to return to his parents in Texas, but he agreed to stay a few days to help his friend brand the cattle. Later, Frank would again need help from his friend when a land dispute began to take place in eastern Wyoming.

With only a few long-horn cattle, Don had not bothered to brand the stock. However, now with a larger herd of the very best cattle from South Dakota, Frank applied for and received permission to use the Circle H brand.

The days and months were long as Frank thought about his days on the Swango ranch and day-dreamed about Virginia. Frank thought to himself, *I wonder if Virginia has finished school and has returned home with her parents.*

Frank's mother Mary Ann could tell that her boy Frank was a bit moody and out-of-sorts. Usually, Frank had a bright smile on his face and was always planning on how to improve the ranch.

Now, however, Frank went about his daily chores with only a half-hearted attempt to keep busy.

Mary Ann thought that Frank would be in better sorts if he would take a trip back to the Swango ranch and visit Virginia. With a little persuasion from both Don and Mary Ann, Frank packed his provisions to ride into South Dakota.

Unlike his first trip into South Dakota with his brother James, this time Frank had a beautiful horse given to him by Mr. Swango, a rifle and his Colt .45. Also, his saddle bags were filled with food. On the back of Frank's saddle he had a bed-roll and a rain slicker.

As Frank approached the Black Hills he was met by a few Sioux Indians. There were only six Indians who had gathered on a hill and followed Frank for almost a half day before they decided to ride down to block Frank's path.

Now Frank had a decision to make. He could either try to outrun the Indian ponies or he could face them and find out what they wanted. Perhaps, Frank could persuade the Indian party to let him pass. As the Indians were not wearing "war paint" Frank thought that perhaps they were just curious and would do no harm.

The Indians could see that Frank had both a rifle and a pistol. The Sioux had only bows and arrows. That is, with the exception of the leader who carried a rifle with eagle war feathers strung along the barrel.

It was a well-known fact that the Sioux had always considered the Black Hills their sacred land. For years the Sioux and Cheyenne Indians had traveled from the prairies to the east into the shelter of the pine covered forest of the Black Hills. The migration began in the late fall in order to spend the unpleasant winters in the Hills and valleys.

It was also known that the buffalo herds wandered into the Hills for protection from the cold and windy prairies. Therefore, the Indians had both protection from the harsh winters and their main food supply.

As more and more white-faces settled in the Hills, the Indians resented their intrusion. After the Indians' defeat by the assigned cavalry, an uneasy peace was established that was to last for a few years.

Reining in his horse Frank dismounted and gave the Sioux the peace sign of an open palm. The Sioux exchanged the greeting and soon the two were sitting on the ground facing each other for a parley. Frank understood a little of the native Sioux language and with hand gestures the two were able to communicate. It seems that the leader of the group had a rifle, but only three remaining bullets for his "long gun."

The chief also stated that it was much easier to bring down a large Bison with a rifle than with bows and arrows. He asked if Frank would trade a few bullets for anything the hunting party had with them on their journey.

As Frank looked over the gathered Indians he viewed little of value that he wanted. However, to keep the peace Frank brought out from his saddle bag a half carton of rifle bullets.

After some discussion, Frank stated that he would give the bullets to the leader carrying the rifle in exchange for an eagle feather and the bone necklace on the leader's chest.

From the corner of his eye, Frank could see that the other Indians snickered at such a one-sided trade. Indeed, the bullets were worth much more than a mere feather and a bone necklace.

But Frank thought that he needed to keep the peace, and, in fact, later the friendship that formed between the two opposing parties became very useful. Frank knew that he would need allies in the upcoming land dispute that was brewing with a few of his father's neighbors.

The Indians shared their food and tobacco and before an hour had passed, such a good relationship developed that Frank asked if the two could become "blood brothers." This resulted from spending almost all of the afternoon in the parley.

To complete the ceremony each man would cut a gash on his right hand and then grip the other so that each man's blood could be exchanged.

It was approaching evening before Frank could continue his journey with the eagle feather sticking out from the band on his hat. From that time on the Sioux in that part of the country called Frank "Eagle Feather."

As the sun was beginning to set, Frank thought that he should find a place to "roll out" his bedroll for the night. After climbing a hill Frank spotted a group of cottonwood trees. He thought that in addition to protecting him from the wind that was always brisk in the open Wyoming prairie, the cottonwood trees growing in a clump in one location usually meant that there would be a small stream to replenish his canteen and have water to brew coffee.

After a peaceful sleep Frank continued his journey to the Swango ranch. As Frank slowly rode east he thought, *I hope that my Mother was right in courting Virginia. What if she already has a steady fellow? Should I turn back before I go any farther?*

"Son, just place your big paw around the outside of the cup. However, if you crush the cup it will cost you the price of one of your calves."

Seth Bullock

Chapter 4

The Swangos

As Frank approached the Swango ranch, it was Virginia who ran to meet him. Frank put his trusty stead to a full gallop. They were very happy to see each other. The first words from Virginia, "Oh, Frank, I thought I would never see you again! I thought about you every day during the last two years I was in school."

Frank, being a bit timid, stated, "Yep, me likewise." With this brief greeting Frank dismounted and hand-in-hand they walked to Virginia's parents' spacious home.

Frank thought to himself, *I sure am glad that I had already established such a good relationship with Virginia's father when I worked for him a couple of years ago.*

As they sat on the Swango's large porch in side-by-side rocking chairs, Mrs. Swango brought them lemonade and fresh-baked cookies to munch on as the two once again became acquainted.

Frank again thought to himself, *If Virginia is half the cook as her mother, and as beautiful as this young filly is, I truly must be in Heaven.* It mattered very little to Frank that Virginia still had the scar on her face where Mr. Gilmore had hit her with his whip.

One of Mr. Swango's ranch hands had taken Frank's horse to the corral, unsaddled the horse and given the horse water and a rub-down. Frank still had the horse given to him by Mr. Swango two years ago.

Frank named the horse "Snip" for a very good reason. Frank yelled out at the cowboy, "Watch out when you try to unsaddle my horse as he will turn his head and give you a good bite."

The ranch hand was about to put Frank's saddle bags in the bunk house when Mr. Swango came off the porch and stated, "Hey, Ed, bring Mr. Hall's personal belongings to the house as he will be staying with us."

After a very fine dinner of beefsteak, the men adjourned to the parlor as Mr. Swango wanted to know how Frank was doing with the fine cattle that were given to him when he departed the ranch. They also enjoyed a glass of cognac and a very fine cigar.

Little was said about the Gilmore shooting and Frank knew better than to ask any questions. Both men ignored the episode that took place in the streets of Rapid City several years ago.

It was well past midnight when Mr. Swango showed Frank his bedroom on the second floor. Mr. Swango reminded Frank that his and Mrs. Swango's bedroom was between his and Virginia's bedroom and that Mrs.

Swango was a very "light" sleeper and hears any noise in the night.

Well, Frank was not going to ruin the beginning of a very good relationship by any indiscretions. Although it was on the mind of both Frank and Virginia wondering what it would be like to be in each other's arms.

The next day Mr. Swango rode with Frank over his many acres as he was justifiably proud of the fine cattle on the ranch. During the long ride Mr. Swango asked Frank, "Just what do you have in mind with my beautiful daughter Virginia?"

Frank gulped and in a very weak voice replied, "Mr. Swango, Virginia and I like each other a whole lot and if it is o.k. with you I would like to ask you for her hand in marriage."

Trying not to display his joy in the answer Mr. Swango stated, "Son, I would be all too happy to add you to the family. You have proved to be an up-right and honest man."

John Swango said that he would very much like for Frank to stay on at his ranch and form a working partnership. Frank didn't answer immediately but after a few moments replied, "Gee, I hadn't thought about this but I bet Virginia would really like that. It would give us some time to find a place to build our own home."

Mr. Swango didn't hesitate but a couple of minutes and agreed to this arrangement. However, he asked, "Do you think your parents could ride in their wagon for a visit to our ranch? That way they will be here for the wedding."

Frank answered, "But while we all are here who would take care of my stock?"

Mr. Swango replied, "I will send a couple of my boys to your ranch to look after things while your parents are in South Dakota."

Frank could hardly contain himself on the ride back to the Swango ranch. He very much wanted to tell Virginia of the good news that her father had approved of their marriage. Truth be known, Mr. Swango and Virginia had discussed this subject even before Frank arrived for his visit.

After arriving back at the Swango ranch both Virginia and Mrs. Swango came out on the porch and gave Frank a big hug. Frank wonders to this day how Mrs. Swango would know of her husband's approval and of Frank asking the question.

As Frank and Virginia wanted to get married as soon as possible it was necessary to notify Frank's parents and make arrangements for them to bring their wagon to the Swango ranch where the wedding was to take place. Unlike the Swango's fancy black buggy, Frank's parents only had the working ranch wagon.

That evening Frank asked Virginia to step into the library of the large home as he needed help in composing a letter to his parents. Frank had very little formal education and needed Virginia's help in writing the letter to his parents. While in the library they had their first long kiss.

Both agreed that this was a good beginning, but both thought that after their marriage they would get much better acquainted.

The two selected wranglers set out to deliver Virginia's letter and stay on the Hall ranch for as long as needed. Before heading out, Mr. Swango gave his two hands very specific instructions that while at the Hall ranch they were to do as much as possible to spruce up the place such as replacing the Hall's front porch, replacing fence posts and any other job that needed to be completed. As the wranglers were used to hard work, and thought they had the best boss in the world, they didn't mind the extra work.

Since Frank had ridden a couple of days across barren prairie he would need new clothes for the wedding. Frank had a roll of cash in his pocket, and he figured he could ride into Belle Fourche and buy a fancy outfit for the wedding. Maybe, just maybe, he would buy a new pair of boots.

Virginia suggested that they take the family buggy into Belle Fourche and together shop for new clothes. Of course, Mrs. Swango would accompany the "love birds." Besides, Virginia wanted her Mother's help in selecting a proper wedding dress.

It was no coincidence that with Frank handling the reins of the horse that Mrs. Swango sat between Frank and Virginia. Mrs. Swango thought that she didn't want these love birds all "hot and bothered" by having their hips touching each other on their buggy ride into Belle Fourche.

Frank was unsure what would be proper dress for the wedding, so it was Mrs. Swango who assisted in not only selecting the wedding dress, but also helping Frank select his suit, shirt and boots.

Frank really didn't have the money to purchase all that Mrs. Swango had selected for him – especially the very fine new pair of boots. It was Virginia's mother who said, "Don't you never mind Frank, as a present to you and our daughter, the Swangos will purchase what you need for the wedding."

After making their purchases, Mrs. Swango thought that all three of them needed a light lunch before heading back to the ranch.

Mrs. Swango led the trio to the Bullock Hotel's spacious and very grand dining room. When completed, the hotel would have three stories consisting of 63 guest rooms. Such a luxury hotel was rare for this part of the west. Seth Bullock and his business partner, Sol Star, would complete this grand hotel in a very short time.

While enjoying their meal, Seth Bullock happened to amble by Mrs. Swango's table. It was obvious to Frank that Mr. Bullock and Mrs. Swango were the very best of friends.

In a very polite gesture Mr. Bullock asked if he could join the group for coffee and dessert. Of course, Mrs. Swango was overjoyed in introducing her soon to be son-in-law to Mr. Bullock.

Frank remembered the manners his mother had taught him and stood to shake Mr. Bullock's hand. Perhaps, due to Frank's nervousness, he griped Mr.

Bullock's right hand with a powerful grip that brought tears to Seth's eyes. It was then that Mr. Bullock stated, "Son, you certainly have a strong hand."

Mr. Bullock was known for his fine sense of humor and stated to Frank, "Son, I notice that with your big hands that you cannot place your index finger in the handle of my very finest teacup that I had imported from France."

Frank was once again embarrassed and said, "Yep, I guess I do have big hands."

This is when Mr. Bullock stated to Frank, "Son, just place your big paw around the outside of the cup. However, if you crush the cup it will cost you the price of one of your calves." Of course Seth Bullock was just jesting with the young fellow and all at the table had a good laugh. That is except Frank, and again he felt his face turning a bright red.

At this point in the conversation Virginia turned to her mother and whispered, "Isn't Frank so cute when he is embarrassed?"

After an extended conversation, there developed a sincere friendship between Frank and Seth Bullock. Within a few months it would become necessary that Frank develop as many influential friends as possible.

Remember also, Frank had established friendship with a group of Sioux Indians on his journey to the Swango ranch. These relationships would also be needed in the years that lay ahead.

Due to Bullock's reputation as an honest man with a fearless personality, the small mining camp was quickly managed without Seth Bullock having to engage in any gunfights.

The Author

Chapter 5

Seth Bullock

Seth Bullock first received his notoriety for becoming the sheriff of Deadwood, South Dakota, following Wild Bill Hickok's murder by Jack McCall. It was Bullock's background as an elected sheriff of Lewis and Clark County in Montana that allowed the citizens of Deadwood to accept Bullock as their sheriff.

Bullock took his job seriously and immediately deputized several locals to enforce the peace. At the time Deadwood had a reputation of being a lawless, rowdy camp. Following Hickok's shooting the good citizens of Deadwood demanded that law and order be established.

Due to Bullock's reputation as an honest man with a fearless personality, the small mining camp was quickly managed without Seth Bullock having to engage in any gunfights.

There was only one enemy whom Bullock had in Deadwood and that was Al Swearengen. Al was the proprietor of the notorious Gem Theater, Deadwood's most notable brothel. Al had a knack for making money from vice and shrewdly invested some of his ill-gotten gains in befriending alliances with Deadwood's wealthy and powerful.

After establishing peace in Deadwood, Bullock brought his wife Martha Eccles Bullock and daughter to town from her parents' home in Michigan. During the Bullocks' time in Deadwood they had another daughter, Florence, and a son, Stanley.

Bullock and his business partner, Sol Star, purchased a ranch where Redwater Creek met the Belle Fourche River and gave it the name of the S & B Ranch Company.

Later Bullock became a deputy U.S. Marshal, partnered with Star and Harris Franklin in the Deadwood Flouring Mill, and invested in mining, the local growth industry. Bullock and Star eventually expanded their business interests to the little bergs of Custer, Sturgis, and Spearfish.

The partners, Star and Bullock contributed further to the economic development of the region by persuading the Fremont, Elkhorn and Missouri Valley Railroad to build a track on their property.

The shrewd partners did this by offering the rail company 40 acres of free right-of-way across their land when a competitive speculator purchased the right-of-way to Minnesela and demanded a high price from the railroad.

The railroad built a station three miles northwest of Minnesela in 1890, and Bullock and Star were instrumental in founding the town of Belle Fourche, offering free lots to anyone who would move from Minnesela.

During this period of time Belle Fourche became the largest railhead for livestock in the United States, and the county seat was changed from Minnesela to Belle Fourche.

In addition to building the fine hotel, Bullock and Star further added to the growth of Belle Fourche.

Due to the railhead, the Swangos now had easy access in shipping their cattle to the markets in Chicago.

It should be known that any friend or family member of the Swangos was now a permanent friend of Seth Bullock. This would bode well for Frank in the long anticipated range war that would take place in a couple of years.

Virginia especially liked Mendelssohn's composition of "Nocture and Wedding March" from *A Midsummer Night's Dream.* She wanted this played at her wedding.

The Author

Chapter 6

The Wedding

On the buggy ride back to the Swango ranch from Belle Fourche the seating arrangement was the same with Frank handling the reins and Mrs. Swango sitting between Frank and Virginia.

Upon returning home Virginia and Mrs. Swango were delighted that Frank's parents had arrived and were already sitting on the grand porch enjoying some lemonade. Immediately, Virginia gave her future mother-in-law a big hug and to Mr. Hall a two-handed handshake.

At first the Halls were startled by Virginia's deep scar that ran along the side of her face. However, after the initial shock, the sweet personality of Virginia made the Halls quickly forget about seeing the ugly scar.

As the men enjoyed refreshments on the porch, the three ladies immediately adjourned to Virginia's upstairs bedroom so that Mrs. Hall could admire the wedding dress.

Mrs. Hall was eager to hear all about Virginia's plan for the wedding. Therefore, Virginia and Mrs. Swango were delighted to share the elaborate plans for the coming event.

As Virginia had attended a very prestigious school in the East, she had taken a number of music courses and fallen in love with a song by the European composer Felix Mendelssohn. Virginia especially liked Mendelssohn's composition of "Nocturne and Wedding March" from the opera *A Midsummer Night's Dream.* She wanted this played at her wedding.

Now the problem was for the selected musicians from Belle Fourche to learn to play the composition. Only one of the musicians could read music. Even though they practiced often, a group of the best fiddle players in this western town could never quite master the complete song.

Therefore, the group settled for a very small part of the selection. This part was later recognized as the traditional *Wedding March.* It was only a few bars from the original score. However, Virginia thought the music was acceptable as her father would escort her to the front of the gathered guests in the rose garden.

While the women were upstairs, the men were visiting on the porch. It was not a surprise to any that Mr. Swango had produced a little whiskey from the parlor to add to the lemonade.

Don Hall stated, "You know this is the best lemon-ade that I have ever tasted. At home in Wyoming we must not have the good water that you have in South Dakota. Perhaps, that is the reason for the improved flavor." Of course, all the men had a good laugh over Don Hall's fine sense of humor.

Mr. Swango thought to himself, *This relationship with the Halls is starting out to be just as I had imagined it would be. With an upstanding young man like Frank, I would expect his parents to be fine people.*

The wedding was to be held on the ranch with a Methodist minister from Belle Fourche officiating. The only members from the Hall family attending would be Frank's parents and Uncle Roy Hall. There were no aunts, cousins or grandparents remaining in the Hall family. The one exception was Don Hall's bachelor brother Roy who operated a cattle ranch in Johnson County, Wyoming.

As it was too far a ride for Frank's friend Tex to attend, he asked his father to serve as his best man. Of course, all of the wranglers on the Swango spread would be attending as well as ranching neighbors and a few influential friends from Belle Fourche.

For sure, Seth Bullock's family, as well as Mr. Bullock's business partners Star and Harris Franklin, would be attending the ceremony. The food for the reception was to be catered from Belle Fourche.

Mrs. Swango's very well-kept rose garden was selected as the site for the wedding. An archway was built and a one-step stage was also constructed for the occasion. The wedding vows were to be read on this stage.

A group of men thoroughly cleaned the barn as this was where the reception was to be held. This meant removing the hay bales and sweeping and painting both the inside and outside of the barn.

Of course, the remainder of the wranglers continued their duties of watching over the large herd of cattle on the vast rangeland owned by the Swangos. As there had always been a large number of coyotes that would love to isolate a young calf, all of the wranglers carried a rifle to shoot the coyotes on site.

Another problem encountered by the cowboys was the numerous prairie dogs that dug holes in the prairie. Many times a horse would stumble into the holes dug by the little varmints and break a leg. Therefore, the cowboys would shoot as many prairie dogs as they could spot.

Finally, the day of the wedding and both Frank and Virginia were nervous. However, Virginia did not let her feelings show as she was so happy that the day had finally arrived.

Frank's father asked his son to step outside on the spacious porch the morning of the wedding to finish their coffee after having a wonderful breakfast prepared by Mrs. Swango and one of her neighbors. Don asked his son, "Do you have a wedding ring for Virginia?"

Frank's face again turned red and stammered, "Oh, Dad I completely forgot about buying a ring."

"Just as I thought, Son, you never were one for the details." However, Don came to the rescue and pulled from his pocket a pure white piece of linen and produced a wedding ring. Don said, "This ring was your Grandmother Hall's ring, and I am sure she would have wanted you to have it."

The very thought of Grandmother Hall produced tears in Frank's eyes as he remembered his Grandmother living on the ranch with the family. Today, the Hall family all had their graves in a plot only a few hundred feet from their main house.

By the afternoon of the wedding all of the participants and hired hands put on their very best clothes. The wranglers even persuaded the old Mexican, Luis Garcia, to take a bath.

Following the wedding ceremony, a group of musicians from Belle Fourche played for the assembled guests in the cleaned-out barn.

Of course, Frank and Virginia were eager to depart for Belle Fourche for their honeymoon. However, all who were gathered for the dance persuaded the "love birds" to stay until sometime after midnight. Frank was careful not to drink much of the "spiked punch" as he was going to drive the Swango buggy into Belle Fourche. Seth Bullock's present to the young couple was a two night stay at his up-scale hotel.

Of course, the wranglers on the Swango ranch did drink the spiked punch and were in a gregarious mood that evening. In fact, a group of cowboys thought it would be fun to follow the couple into Belle Fourche and harass them outside their hotel.

As the newlyweds pulled out of the ranch in the buggy heading to Belle Fourche, the cowboys saddled their horses and were right behind the buggy. However, about a mile down the dusty road they were met by Seth Bullock and John Swango. Mr. Swango told his boys, "Now you all turn around and head back to the bunk house. You are not going to spoil the first evening that my lovely daughter has with Frank."

Without any hesitation, the cowboys headed back to the ranch. After all, there was still more punch to drink and fiddle music to listen to.

Frank and Virginia were not concerned that the Bullock Hotel had not been completely finished. The first floor had been partly finished to include a dining room, tea room and a couple of elaborately furnished guest bedrooms.

Of course, Mr. Bullock had reserved one of the guest bedrooms for the newlyweds. Seth Bullock even had his hotel staff place a large bouquet of roses in the room. In addition, a large bottle of the very finest champagne imported from France was sitting in an ice bucket beside the large bed.

Virginia loved the taste of the champagne. However, Frank had about a half glass and decided that his taste wasn't quite as sophisticated as his new bride's. But rather than call for room service and have a bottle of whiskey delivered to the room, Frank decided he had drank enough of the spiked punch at the reception to last for one evening.

Late the next morning there was a soft knock at the hotel door and a nice looking young man had brought a breakfast tray to the room. Now Frank had never eaten his breakfast in bed. In fact, he thought of people eating in bed was the height of laziness.

This was to be the first time that Frank and Virginia had a slight disagreement. So far their relationship was as close to perfect as possible. In an attempt to keep it that way, the idea of eating in bed was never discussed again.

When General Nelson Miles learned all the details of the massacre he immediately relieved Colonel James W. Forsyth of command.

The Author

Chapter 7

The Wounded Knee Massacre

John Swango was always in the need for new wranglers for his ever increasing herd of cattle. As was the nature of cowboys in the 1800's, a few men would drift through South Dakota on their journey to Montana or Wyoming to either seek better employment or in hopes of starting their own spreads.

In early January of 1890, a drifter stopped by the Swango ranch to both seek warmth and perhaps a job as he had spent most of his money gambling in Dead-wood.

Mr. Swango met the very cold cowboy on the steps of his grand home and the two men walked to Swango's bunkhouse as it was just about time for the cowhands to have their evening meal.

Cliff Alexander, the drifter, was very happy for a chance to get warm by the bunkhouse stove and also very pleased that one of Swango's men volunteered to take Cliff's horse to the enclosed barn to unsaddle, rub down, and feed the animal. As the horse was in bad condition from the long day on the trail, one of Swango's cowhands even provided a horse blanket to throw over the animal.

After enjoying the typical meal of beans, cornbread, bacon and pie, the wranglers were eager to hear what had been happening outside the confines of the ranch.

Cliff was willing to tell the assembled men, including John Swango, the horrible massacre that had happened on the Lakota Pine Ridge Indian Reservation. John Swango especially had good relations with the Indians in the area and was very annoyed with what Cliff was reporting.

It seems that on December 28th a detachment of the U.S. 7th Cavalry Regiment intercepted a band of Miniconjou Lakota and Hunkpapa Lakota Indians near Porcupine Butte. The Cavalry orders were to escort them five miles westward to Wounded Knee Creek where they were to make camp. After both Indians and soldiers had settled for the night, the remainder of the 7th Cavalry Regiment arrived. Colonel James Forsyth immediately surrounded the encampment and brought up the regiment's four Hotchkiss guns.

The next morning the troops were ordered to enter the Indians' camp to disarm the Lakota Indians. Evidently, one Indian would not surrender his rifle. The Indian, by the name of Black Coyote, protested vigorously as he told the soldiers that he needed the rifle to hunt bison and other game to feed his family.

When the enlisted soldier was not able to grab the rifle from Black Coyote, an accidental shot was fired which resulted in the trooper opening fire on the Indians.

The soldiers surrounding the gathered Indians, shot and killed not only the armed braves, but also women and children. The undisciplined troopers even accidently killed a few of their own men. Later documents claim that twenty-five troopers were killed.

Not knowing what would happen next, the warriors who still had weapons immediately returned fire at the attacking troopers. It was reported later that several U.S. cavalrymen pursued and killed many who were unarmed.

Although the War Department wanted to cover-up this unfortunate incident, they reported that just a few Indians were killed. Later a reporter for a Rapid City newspaper discovered the truth that over 300 Indians had died.

What really angered John Swango was that twenty troopers were awarded the coveted Medal of Honor. As John Swango's son-in-law had made friends of an Indian Chief, he wanted to contact Frank to find the name of his "Blood Brother." As the weather conditions prevented sending for Frank, the news of the massacre would have to wait until better weather.

Swango's men wanted to know more of the details. However, Cliff had only gossip from other gamblers in Deadwood about the aftermath of the shootings.

One of the men at Cliff's gambling table told how there was a three-day blizzard following the massacre, and when the storm abated that the officer in charge had hired civilians to bury the dead Indians.

The burial party found the Indians frozen and so the men merely threw the remains in a common grave on a hill overlooking the encampment.

It was reported that one of the civilians working on the burial had seen four infants, all alive, wrapped in their deceased mothers' shawls.

When General Nelson Miles learned of all the details of the massacre, he immediately relieved Colonel James W. Forsyth of command. An exhaustive Army Court of Inquiry convened by Miles criticized Forsyth for his tactical blunder, but otherwise exonerated him of responsibility. It is still unclear why the Court of Inquiry did not conduct a formal court-martial.

Ironically, the Secretary of War concurred with the decision and reinstated Forsyth to command the 7th Cavalry. Testimony had indicated that for the most part, troops attempted to avoid non-combatant casualties. General Miles continued to protest against the absence of court-martial hearings as he believed that Colonel Forsyth had deliberately disobeyed his commands in order to destroy the Indians.

When John Swango later learned that James Forsyth was promoted to Major General, he sent off a series of letters to the War Department in which Mr. Swango used somewhat disrespectful language criticizing the decisions made in both the massacre and especially the promotion of James Forsyth.

The conflict at Wounded Knee did not end the multi-century series of problems which existed between the U.S. and American Indians.

It seems that there was an armed confrontation between Lakota warriors and the United States Army on December 30, 1890. Again, the conflict happened on the Pine Ridge Indian Reservation the day after the major battle.

The fight occurred on White Clay Creek that was about 15 miles north of Pine Ridge. The cavalry found Sioux Indians fleeing from the continued hostile situation surrounding the battle at Wounded Knee.

Company K of the 7th Cavalry was sent to force the Lakotas to return to the reservations where they were assigned. Some of the Indians were Brule Lakota from the Rosebud Indian Reservation.

After some careless tactics, Company K found themselves pinned down in a valley by the combined Lakota forces and had to be rescued by the 9th Cavalry.

The 9th Cavalry was an all-African American regiment. The Indians on the plains called these soldiers Buffalo Soldiers. Perhaps, because the soldiers often wore buffalo robes to keep warm or the more popular idea is that the soldiers were black like the buffalo.

History will document that a Lakota warrior by the name of Plenty Horses shot and killed Army Lieutenant Edward W. Casey, commandant of the Cheyenne Scouts.

The testimony introduced at the trial of Plenty Horses and his subsequent acquittal also helped cancel the legal culpability of the United States Army for the Wounded Knee Massacre.

Chapter 8

The Johnson County War in Wyoming

Upon returning back to the Swango ranch from Belle Fourche one evening, Frank's buggy was met by one of the Roy Hall's wranglers. The news must have been important as the cowboy had his trusty steed in full gallop.

Henry pulled up his horse and said to Frank, "I'm afraid I have bad news for you. It seems that your uncle Roy has had a run-in with gun slingers hired by the Wyoming Stock Growers Association."

Frank inquired if his uncle had been shot and the wrangler said, "As far as I know the gunslingers only gave Roy a warning that he was not to participate in the spring branding of his herd of cattle."

As a background to the troubles that the small-time ranchers were having in Johnson County on the Montana border, one needs to know the history of the late 1800's and early 1900's.

This was a time of conflict over land use in Johnson County. The resulting outright war that resulted was among the worst in the episodes of the West.

During the late 1800's most of Wyoming was public domain, meaning the land was open to homesteaders and to open range stock grazing. British, East Coast and other investors poured a lot of money into huge herds of cattle that were turned loose on the open range.

In the spring, the ranchers would have a roundup and separate the cows and calves and brand all the new calves. Quite often, before the roundup began in earnest, orphan and stray calves would disappear and be quietly branded.

The larger ranch owners called this "cattle rustling." They were very aggressive against it, going so far as to forbid their own wranglers from owning any cattle and threatening to lynch anyone else they didn't like.

Under the doctrine of Prior Appropriation (first to settle the land) and the size of the herd, big and small ranchers sorted out their cattle and usually respected the property and use rights.

However, at times the larger rancher would "claim" huge tracts of public land and stop newcomers and homesteaders from coming in.

Most of the large cattle ranchers organized themselves as the Wyoming Stock Growers Association. As these were some of Wyoming's wealthiest and most popular residents, the Association held great political power.

They also organized the cattle industry by scheduling roundups and sending their cattle shipments by rail. To no one's surprise they employed outsiders to investigate any cattle rustling against their members. To stay on the side of the law the wealthy ranchers called these outside gunslingers "a regulated detective agency."

Frank's Uncle Roy had participated in the annual roundup for years without any trouble. However, after a previous hot and very dry summer, thousands of cattle starved to death the following winter that produced very cold and snow-covered ranges.

The next spring following the very harsh winter the larger ranchers banded together and took control of even larger parcels of land and started to regulate water flows and supplies in the area.

These large land owners went so far as to chase small homesteaders off their own property and then burn down their buildings. During the spring roundup they excluded the smaller ranchers in the area from participating by labeling them all cattle rustlers.

As Roy owned a very small herd of cattle, he was among the ranchers who faced trouble with the established wealthy of the area.

It was during this "face-off" that Roy had dispatched one of his workers to the Swango ranch to ask his nephew for help. Roy knew he needed help when two of his neighbors – Ella Watson and Jim Averell, two small homesteaders, were lynched by riders working for one of the large cattle ranches.

It seems the two were innocent of the claims of "rustling" but several witnesses to the lynching disappeared completely while others were either heavily intimidated or found dead in suspicious circumstances.

During this time period several more dubious lynching's happened, and to make matters even worse, not a single individual was ever tried or convicted of any of the killings.

Roy Hall and a group of other small ranchers formed their own Northern Wyoming Farmers and Stock Growers Association. Of course, this meant that they were immediately threatened by the members of the larger Wyoming Stock Growers Association.

The group of smaller ranchers let others in the area know that they would be holding their own roundup in the spring of 1892.

The large stockholders immediately hired 23 hired gunslingers from the Paris, Texas area. They also hired four new cattle detectives. To make matters worse a state senator and the state water commissioner joined with them to intimidate the smaller ranchers.

The cards were really stacked against the smaller ranchers when a respected surgeon, a local newspaper editor and a reporter for the *Chicago Herald* sided with the larger stockholders.

This group of bullies was led by Frank Canton, himself a former bank robber and cattle rustler. Later Canton turned lawman before once again reverting to his old ways and became a gun for hire.

Canton was given a list of 70 people who were supposed to be either shot or hanged and a list of ranches that were to be burned.

With authorization from the larger ranchers, Canton had a contract with the Texans to pay $5 per day, together with a $50 bounty for every "rustler" he killed. This contract expanded to include killing ranchers as far away as Casper and Douglas. This nasty group was known as the "Walcott's Regulators."

Little did the Regulators know at the time that Frank's best friend from Texas, Tex Bennett, had joined the group from Paris, Texas?

Tex thought that if he was on the "inside" he could warn his friend Frank the plans of the Regulators. In fact, it was Tex who had one of his friends ride into the Swango ranch to warn Frank that his uncle was going to be in big trouble. Now that both Tex's friend and a wrangler who worked for Uncle Roy had given Frank the message that there was trouble in Wyoming, Frank knew he needed to organize a group of cowboys to assist his uncle.

Before the cowboys on the Swango ranch could get organized and also enlist a group of gunfighters of their own, the havoc started in Wyoming.

Walcott's Regulators gathered in Cheyenne took a specially hired train to Casper and then proceeded to Johnson County on horseback. They cut telegraph lines along the way so that no news could get out. The group's first target was Nate Champion, one of the organizers of the Northern Wyoming Farmers and Stock Growers Association.

It was on Saturday, April 9, 1892, that the group completed its daring deed and killed Champion and four other people in Champion's cabin. After killing Champion and his companions, they set the cabin on fire.

It was said that the Regulators pinned a note on the chest of Champion that read "Cattle Thieves Beware," and left the grisly site.

Two cowboys looking for stray cattle came upon the murdered men and told rancher Jack Flagg about what they saw. Flagg rode to the county seat in Buffalo and told the sheriff.

On Monday morning, the sheriff, with a posse of about 200 men, caught up with the "Regulators" and as a result a long gun battle followed at a log barn on the TA Ranch by Crazy Woman Creek.

During the gun battle, three of the Texans were killed. Somehow, a few of the Texans escaped and got a message off to the acting Governor of Wyoming who telegraphed President Benjamin Harrison for assistance in helping the "Regulars" escape.

The Secretary of War ordered the 6th Cavalry from Fort McKinney to go to the TA Ranch and take custody of the "Regulators." The Cavalry arrived just as the posse was preparing to burn the barn down with all the Texas gunmen inside.

The troopers from the Cavalry took the "Regulators" to Cheyenne where they were held at the barracks of Fort D.A. Russell. The Johnson County attorney started to gather evidence, including the list of men who were to be killed. The list was found in one of the gunmen's saddle bags.

According to *The Times* on April 23, "The evidence is said to implicate more than twenty prominent stockmen of Cheyenne whose names have not been mentioned."

It was also rumored that several wealthy stockmen of Omaha as well as men high in authority in the State of Wyoming were guilty. They would all be charged with aiding and abetting the invasion, and warrants were issued to arrest all of them.

Well, it never happened. The charges against the politicians were never filed. The Texans were released on bail and they all disappeared. Then when Johnson County couldn't afford the costs of prosecution, all other charges were dropped.

It seems that all of this happened before Frank Hall and others could muster enough men to come to the aid of his uncle.

The good news was that Roy Hall survived the war. Like the other small ranchers in the area he continued to operate his small "spread."

However, the sod-busters or better known as homesteaders never did return in large numbers. Perhaps, this was due to the realization that the sod in Wyoming was too poor to farm.

As far as Frank knew, Tex never did participate in the killings and made his escape back to Texas prior to the gun fight with Champion.

As the buggy came over a rise, the couple found a beautiful setting between two pine covered hilltops. The valley between the hills was ideal and both agreed that indeed this would be the perfect spot for their new home.

The Author

Chapter 9

The Cattle Ranches in Northwest South Dakota

Frank was eager to tell both his father and Mr. Swango of the trouble his uncle was experiencing in Wyoming. Of course, Don was concerned about his brother Roy. After consulting Mr. Swango the two men started their plan on how to face the "Regulators" if they too had an encounter.

However, prior to gathering their own guns-for-hire and organizing a raid into Wyoming the news reached them that the 6th Cavalry from Fort McKinney had resolved the problem and the "Regulators" were all in custody.

The wedding of Frank and Virginia had brought the elder Halls and Swangos together many times. Respect, admiration and trust united the two families. One evening after the six of them had enjoyed a fine meal, John stated that they had something important to discuss. As was usually the custom in those days, the men adjourned to the study to discuss the future of both the newlyweds and the ranches in Wyoming.

With considerable surprise to both Don and Frank Hall, it was John Swango who told them that he had out bid another group of ranchers and purchased a vast amount of good grazing pasture that adjoined the Swango spread.

It was with the assistance of Seth Bullock and his partner's money that they were able to purchase this valuable range land. The spread of very good pasture land extended from Belle Fourche north to the North Dakota border and south to the edge of Spearfish. To the east the land stretched over one-hundred fifty miles. The Swangos already owned all the ground up to the edge of the Wyoming state line.

The plan that the Swangos, along with Bullock and his business partners, had in mind was to bring the entire Hall family into a partnership on this large holding of land.

This would mean that Frank's parents and Uncle Roy could sell their small holdings and move onto the ranch land in South Dakota.

The Halls and especially Frank were exceedingly happy and at the same time humbled by the generous offer from their new friends in South Dakota. John Swango had another reason for extending the invitation, and that was that he was especially close to his daughter Virginia and could not bear the thought of her living far from home.

To Seth Bullock and his partners, this was purely a very smart business deal now that the railroad was operating out of Belle Fourche. Seth's business partners had met the Halls and Frank at the wedding of Frank and Virginia.

Over a glass of Mr. Bullock's very best imported cognac they all agreed that the Hall family could be trusted, and they could sense that the Halls were very serious and hard-working people.

As Roy Hall had survived the ranch war in Wyoming, he had no trouble selling his small herd of cattle and humble shack of a home to the large land holders who were his neighbors.

Anyway, it was either sell or be burned out by the "Regulators." True, the group of Texans had been arrested, but the Halls knew that it wouldn't be long until the wealthy cattle barons would hire another group of outlaws to terrorize the smaller cattlemen and the few homesteaders who remained in the area.

Suffering a loss, Frank's parents sold their land and buildings. The wranglers from the Swango ranch drove the cattle across the Wyoming border to Hall's new ranch in South Dakota.

Remembering the good relations that Frank had established with the Sioux hunting party, the cowboys from the Swango ranch had an escort back to the South Dakota ranch.

The wranglers could see that two rows of Sioux warriors rode beside the herd. One row of Indians rode parallel to the north while a few others rode parallel to the south. Frank had somehow forgotten to mention to the Swango wranglers his encounter with the Sioux. So on the entire ride back into South Dakota the cowboys thought the Indians might attack the group.

Upon hearing the story of the Indian parley with Frank and now understanding they were in no danger, the cowboys felt justifiably angry. It was a mistake for Frank to laugh at the story of how Swango's cowboys thought they needed a double guard on the herd the first night.

In fact, they were so angry that they chased Frank down and dunked him in the stream running by the bunk house. They also proceeded to roll him in the mud beside the stream.

Frank was not going to reveal what he was thinking. *If the Swango hired hands only knew that there were only ten Indians at the most and all but one was armed with nothing but their bows and arrows, they really would be mad. Their chief, although holding a repeating rifle probably did not have any remaining bullets. This was because they were most likely used in hunting the buffalo.*

Ordinarily Mr. Swango would defend his new son-in-law, but this time he thought that the young lad needed a lesson. Anyway, everyone had a good laugh and also relieved that the Hall family was safe.

It should be known that the Swango family, Seth Bullock and his business partners retained the title to the newly purchased land. That is except for a few acres where Roy, Frank's parents and the young couple decided to build their new homes.

Everyone was happy with the new arrangement and for once the Hall family felt safe and now had a bright future with a fine herd of cattle primarily supplied by Mr. Swango. All of the profits from the sale of the Hall cattle would remain with Don, Mary Ann, Frank, Virginia and Roy.

Since Frank and Virginia had been living with her parents since returning from their short honeymoon, it was now time for them to take the family buggy and scour the countryside looking for just the right location to build their dream house.

Virginia hated the wide-open spaces where her family lived as snow drifted against the house and outbuildings in the winter and it was hot with no shade in the summer. Mrs. Swango attempted many times to grow trees, but they needed water and the hired help frequently forgot to water the young trees after they were planted.

Virginia loved the Black Hills and so the couple traveled south toward the newly formed little berg of Spearfish, South Dakota. Frank reminded Virginia that he needed room for the house, barn and other outbuildings.

As the buggy came over a rise, the couple found a beautiful setting between two pine covered hilltops. The valley between the hills was ideal, and both agreed that indeed this would be the perfect spot for their new home.

Frank thought that their new ranch house would be far enough away from the Swangos that Virginia' s mother would not be on their front porch every day. Yet, the location would be less than a half day's ride between homes.

The neighbors all pitched in to help in the construction of the home. Also, Mr. Swango could afford to assign a couple of his best men to help.

By 1893 a corporation by the name of Sears, Roebuck and Company was founded in Chicago, Illinois. The partners, Richard Sears and Alva C. Roebuck, knew that farmers and ranchers often brought their crops and cattle to the city to be sold. After making their sale, the farmers and ranchers would buy what they needed, then they would ship the supplies to their homes – part of the way by train.

By 1894, Richard Sears and Alva Roebuck published a Sears Catalog that at times numbered 322 pages in length. The catalog would feature such items as sewing machines, bicycles and a host of other new items.

By the following year dolls, icebox refrigerators, cook-stoves, and groceries had been added to the catalog. Virginia had found a Sears Catalog in Bullock's Hotel and thought that there were many items that would complete their home.

As the railroad came directly from Chicago to Belle Fourche, the answer to her prayers had been given. After arriving on the railroad platform, their farm wagon could bring the selected items to their ranch home near Spearfish.

Virginia's father surprised her by paying for an icebox, sewing machine and cook-stove. Virginia had learned to sew on her mother's sewing machine and had made most of her dresses. Now she planned to even make the drapes and curtains for their new home.

One evening Frank was exhausted as he had been cleaning the barn and placing new fence posts around the corral. After washing for supper he noticed that Virginia seemed to be much happier than usual. She also had a bright glow about her face.

After supper with Frank helping Virginia with the dishes, Virginia asked Frank to step into their sewing room to see what she had been making that afternoon.

Frank picked up a very small blanket and stated, "It seems that you still have more work to complete this blanket. Do you plan to place several pieces together to make a much larger blanket? Also, why did you select such a bright color of blue for the blanket?"

Virginia beamed and said to Frank, "That is all the larger the blanket needs to be to cover a baby."

Frank then asked, "Which one of our neighbors is having a baby?"

Virginia answered, "Have you not been noticing that I have gained a little weight this summer?"

Frank replied, "Well, yes but I was not going to mention it so as not to nag you about eating so much."

"Well," replied Virginia, "I have been eating for two now."

As usual Frank's face turned its usual red and he stammered, "Gosh, how did that happen?"

Virginia answered, "The same way we have new calves in the spring."

Finally, Frank understood and started a jig around the living room before grabbing Virginia and whirling her around the room with him. Virginia was also happy, but had to caution Frank that he needed to be a bit gentler now that she was expecting.

As usual Frank was somewhat embarrassed by his next question when he rather timidly asked, "Gosh, Virginia can we still do it?"

Virginia loved to tease Frank and replied, "What do you mean Frank by do it?"

Finally, before they went to bed that night Virginia explained to Frank that yes they could "still do it" for a few more months. However, as Frank was a very big man some adjustment would need to be made when they were under the sheets.

In the middle of the night Frank woke up Virginia with a couple of questions, "Virginia, have you told your mother or my mother?"

Virginia was not happy about being nudged awake, but replied, "No Frank you are the first to know, now go back to sleep."

Chapter 10

The Hall Dynasty Expands

Meanwhile, to the east Frank's Uncle Roy had found a location he thought would make a good place to build his house. The ground already had a good stand of prairie grass and the few people in the unincorporated little town of Faith stated that water could be found by digging wells. Also, many in the area had dug earthen dams that would soon fill when the winter snow melted and the sparse spring rains began in early April.

When John Swango and Seth Bullock had heard that Roy had selected this location, it was Seth who stated, "I understand the spread you have decided upon is just a few miles west of Faith. I believe that you will need faith to live out on this isolated prairie land."

However, Roy perhaps had the last laugh. He knew that the founder of the little berg of Faith, by the name of Faith Rockefeller, had invested in having the railroad come all the way west to end at Faith. The rail was the permanent end of the railroad, a local spur off the Milwaukee Road Railroad. It took until 1912 to have the small town incorporated. This information about the building of the rail line to this location was given to him by one of Seth Bullock's business partners, Sol Star.

By having the rail line end in Faith, Roy could ship his cattle to the eastern markets such as Omaha, Nebraska and Chicago, Illinois.

With help from new friends, Roy soon had a small house built on his property just a few miles outside the town of Faith.

Roy's brother worried about his bachelor brother living by himself so many miles from civilization. However, Roy quickly made friends with his neighbors and would occasionally ride into Faith to buy supplies he needed for his ranch.

On one such Saturday morning, Roy was enjoying a cup of coffee at the only café in Faith, when a rather attractive lady came into the café for her noon meal. As there were no other patrons in the little café, Roy ambled over to the lady's table and introduced himself. From the corner of his eye he could see the cook and only waitress smiling.

It seems that this lady was one of only two widows in town. Sarah Cummings had lost her husband nearly two years ago in a ranching accident when he attempted to break a saddle horse and had been thrown against a corral post and crushed by the falling horse.

Sarah had difficulty making ends meet as she had two teenage boys to raise. Although the boys were very helpful on the ranch, Sarah had little money to spare. However, on this particular day she had treated herself to a lunch at the café.

Roy was ordinarily a very shy man but when he eyed this cute little button of a lady all inhibitions disappeared and he thought to himself, *What would I have to lose if I present myself in a very polite and gentlemanly way to this young filly.*

After introducing themselves, Sarah invited Roy to sit with her while she enjoyed her lunch. When she had finished, Roy very much wanted to extend the conversation and so offered to buy Sarah a piece of pie and a cup of coffee.

Sarah had eyed the fresh baked peach pie as she entered the café and thought that she could not afford to buy the dessert for herself. Therefore, she was delighted to accept Roy's gift.

The couple spent over an hour talking before Sarah excused herself and stated, "Roy, I hope that I see you again. It seems that we have a lot in common."

With this announcement Roy blushed and standing stated, "Yes, Sarah I will look forward to our next meeting."

Sarah exited the café before Roy. This gave Roy the opportunity to quiz the waitress about his new-found friend. Roy was delighted to learn Sarah was not married. Maybe he should visit Faith more often in hopes of getting to know Sarah better and even getting the nerve to take her for a buggy ride.

Of course, since Roy had ridden into town on his ranch horse, he needed to purchase a buggy and perhaps a horse trained to pull a buggy. Prior to leaving Faith, Roy made his way to the only livery stable in town in the hopes of purchasing the appropriate buggy. There was only one horse trained to pull a buggy and so Roy also purchased the horse.

As was the custom in those early days, the buggy was black and had a fringe around the top of the carriage. The owner of the livery stable even gave Roy a new whip to complete the transaction.

Roy might have been a little worried as he bought the only horse remaining in the stable. However, he was not disappointed as he rode back to his ranch. It seemed that this horse had been trained much like a "Tennessee Walking Horse" where the horse's front and back legs on one side moved together giving a very smooth ride.

Roy was very proud of his new buggy and horse. He tied his trusty stead, Silver, to the back of the buggy and with great glee made his way back to the ranch.

In the following months Roy and Sarah met several times at the café and Roy had taken Sarah for a buggy ride in the country.

It was only the third date when Sarah asked Roy to stop by for an evening meal and meet her two boys. The first meeting with Sarah's two boys, John and Harry, went better than Roy had expected.

The two boys were very polite and thrilled to see their mother so happy after two years living without a man around the house. On future buggy trips the two boys came along with the couple.

As Sarah was only five feet four inches tall with curly red hair and freckles, Roy started calling her "Button." Sarah didn't mind the nickname. In fact, although she would never let Roy know, she thought the name was sort of cute.

Both boys had curly red hair passed along from their mother. John was about fourteen years old and his younger brother about twelve.

Roy was an expert with rope tricks, and taught the two boys how to twirl a rawhide rope and to lasso a post on the corral gate. Roy told the boys that he would help in branding the newborn calves in the spring. Roy also made himself useful in completing small chores around Sarah's ranch.

Roy taught the two boys how to properly shoot with a rifle. They became quite proficient and in fact probably better marksmen than Roy. In later years, the proficiency with a rifle would come in handy as trouble in Europe might mean that the United States would become involved.

It took only a couple of months for Roy to propose to Sarah. Sarah and the boys were so happy that now Roy would become part of their family. Sarah and Roy worshipped each other and the citizens of Faith could tell when they saw the two holding hands while walking down the main street that this was a match made in Heaven.

Since Sarah's two boys were in their teens, they decided to keep their father's name of Cummings rather than being adopted by Roy Hall.

Even though John and Harry were not really part of the Hall family clan, they were readily accepted as such and always included in family affairs.

Sarah and Roy planned on a church wedding in Faith. When his nephew Frank and very pregnant wife Virginia visited, the news made everyone very happy and all of the Swangos planned on attending.

The newly married couple decided to sell Sarah's ranch that was just outside the town of Faith. Driving Sarah's cattle through the main street of Faith was a sight to see. The move was successful and none of the cattle managed to escape the wranglers and made it to Roy's ranch.

Roy, Frank and several others built two more rooms on to Roy's existing home to make it more comfortable for a growing family, and soon to be prosperous family. After a few years of living with Roy and Button both John and Harry married local girls and bought their own ranches.

Chapter 11

Winter Blizzards on the Plains

The snow blizzards were severe in the mid-1800 and early 1900's. The storms that caused the most damage were ones where the cattlemen lost vast herds of their livestock.

Usually the worst storms struck in January. Similar to the earlier storms, the weeks before usually were pleasant. However, in the windswept prairies of South Dakota storms were unpredictable. It was true that snow remained on the ground between snowstorms, but the wind and cold temperatures were not a factor in getting the children to school.

The ranchers in the area always thinned their large herds of cattle in the fall in this part of the state. It was just too expensive to feed the cattle over the sometimes very long winters.

Those remaining herds of cattle were driven to the safety of the cottonwood trees close to the creeks on each rancher's property. A few of the ranchers even built log windbreaks for the cattle to huddle behind. The cattle were fed hay brought to them in either wagons or by large sleds through the deep snow.

On Frank and Virginia's ranch the horses in the corral had to be fed and the water in their large tanks had to be kept ice free and filled at all times. This was true on all ranches on the prairie.

Frank was very prudent and had cut and stored a vast quantity of wood to keep the cooking stove and large fireplace going. Even with temperatures outside sliding down below zero for entire nights and much of the next days, the house was comfortable. These two heat sources would be all the ranchers had to keep their homes warm in the coldest months of the winter.

A combination of gale winds, blinding snow and rapidly dropping temperatures made these storms all the more dangerous. Virginia would pile rugs and blankets around the windows and doors in an attempt to keep the wind from blowing into the home.

As the well handles were often frozen shut, Frank would wade through many feet of snow drifts to the stream that was about twenty to thirty yards from their back door to bring pails of water to the house.

On one such winter morning Frank and Virginia woke at dawn as was their habit, but were unable to see outside. Frank said to Virginia, "I must go to the corral to check on our horses and break the ice on their water tank. Also, I need to be sure they have plenty of hay for a few days as this storm could get worse."

The danger of leaving the house was that with the blinding snow Frank might not be able to find his way back. Therefore, Frank tied a rope around his waist and let the rope out as he waded through the large snow drifts to the corral. After breaking the ice with an axe and pitching hay into the closed portion of the barn, he followed the rope back to the house.

During these winter months luck would be with the children in the scattered rural schools dotting the prairie. If there would be some warning of the approaching storm, the parents could quickly bring their children home on horseback. Some days the children couldn't get to school at all.

Many of the teachers in the one-room schools were brought to various ranches to wait out the storms. Many ranch homes had only one bedroom so the teacher would pile blankets beside the fireplace usually found in the middle of the largest room in the house.

It was the custom on the ranches in the prairie states for the women to can vegetables and even meat in the summer months in order to exist on this food in the sometimes very long winters.

As storms would often extend for over six weeks at a time, many of the families would run dangerously low on food. It would be difficult for the men to hunt in such conditions as most of the animals had also hunkered down into deep burrows to stay alive.

Typically, there would be a break in the winter weather about the middle of February and then it was time for the men to take their ice saws and cut large chunks of ice from their dams to place in the earthen cellars that each rancher had on his property.

Usually, a group of neighbors would help each other in this tedious and dangerous job. The idea of breaking the ice chunks and hauling the ice to the earthen cellars was to insure that there would be ample ice in the summer months.

The cellars were usually about twenty feet away from the main house. The men would layer the ice chunks with a mat of straw to help slow thawing in the summer.

By having the ice in the earthen cellars, the women could keep their "iceboxes" cold in order to store milk, butter and meat.

Since the neighbors had taken care of each other, then Frank and Virginia would check on their parents and Uncle Roy.

To the relief of everyone, most of the hardy pioneers on the prairie would survive the winter's blast of weather. Perhaps a few of their cattle did not make it through the difficult winters, but usually there would be no casualties among the many ranchers.

Chapter 12

The Last of the Train Robbers

A number of brazen stagecoach hold-ups happened when the Deadwood to Cheyenne stagecoach line transported gold from the Black Hills to Cheyenne.

However, with the advent of the railroad the unsavory bandits would now have a harder time robbing from the fast moving trains. Nevertheless, there were still men who thought they could be successful in pulling off a robbery.

One story was that six men were working as cowboys and were hired to take a herd of cattle from Texas to a market in Kansas. Once the cattle were sold the men made their way to Deadwood, South Dakota, and together lost all of the cattle owner's money playing poker,

Not daring to go back to Texas without the boss's money, the cowboys began to rob stage coaches and later attempted to rob trains.

The leader of the group by the name of Ivan Hutchinson knew that the train running between Chicago and Belle Fourche carried large amounts of money. Therefore, he convinced his motley crew to attempt to rob this particular train. The group decided to rob the train on the return run from Chicago. They thought they had a better chance of escaping into the Black Hills or down into the Badlands just to the east of the Black Hills.

The plan was to first capture the station master and destroy the telegraph. The next step was to signal a westbound express train to stop. The six bandits then boarded the train.

The six men made their way from the passenger car to the mail car in the hopes of breaking open the safe they expected to find in the mail car. Finding only about $500 in the mail car safe, they proceeded to rob the larger safe, but it had a time lock preventing it from being opened until the train reached Belle Fourche.

A few of the train robbers were despicable individuals. On this particular robbery one of the desperadoes viciously beat the express messenger in an attempt to get him to open the larger safe. However, although suffering an extreme beating, he was not able to open the safe. The six men continued to search the mail car and did find some wooden boxes which revealed freshly minted gold pieces worth at least $70,000. To this day no one can explain why these gold pieces were not in the safe.

The bandits were still not satisfied with their haul and proceeded to systematically rob the train passengers. As a result of this robbery they escaped with an unknown amount of cash and valuables such as gold watches and jewelry taken from the ladies on the train.

The robbers stopped the train and escaped by having a seventh man waiting with horses at a bridge trellis. It was agreed upon while planning the heist that they would ride off in different directions after splitting the profits.

The robbers stopped the train just outside Belle Fourche so that the riders could escape into the hills and valleys of the Black Hills. At least three of the bandits made a bee line east to head into the barren Badlands.

A very costly mistake the robbers made was that during the robbery of the train passengers, one of the masked men struck one of Seth Bullock's best friends on the head. The attack was so brutal that upon arriving in Belle Fourche, Seth's friend was not expected to live.

Seth was planning on meeting his friend who had traveled from Chicago, and when Travis did not climb down from the train, Seth boarded the train to find a couple of ladies attempting to revive him.

Immediately, Seth took Travis to the local doctor and then proceeded to form a posse. Not knowing which direction to follow, the posse decided to ride to the east as there were horse prints where the desperados had jumped the train and rode off on horseback. The horses were easy to track as there had been a heavy rain the day before the robbery.

Riding all night and into the next day the posse could not catch up with the hard riding robbers. However, stopping at numerous ranches along the way the posse knew they were heading in the right direction as several ranchers had noticed horsemen riding hard past their homes at night. The ranchers knew that riding a horse hard in the night was dangerous and not attempted by many cowboys.

Finally, at the last little berg by the name of Wall, South Dakota, the posse knew that the robbers were headed straight into the barren Badlands. This would be another mistake the train robbers made as they probably did not know just how desolate this area would be. If they expected to fill their canteens from any streams, they would be disappointed as there would be little or no water in the Badlands.

Seth Bullock had selected a "tracker" to accompany the posse and after some searching, the trail was picked up and followed. However, Seth and the other members of the posse had sense enough to fill their canteens with water while in Wall. The men bought two more canteens, making a total of three canteens per man, before heading after the robbers. The posse also had brought extra horses so that each horse would not be exhausted by the long ride. Every few miles the posse would change horses.

Seth had a good plan in pursuing the now desperate train bandits. Seth's plan was to select one of the best sharpshooters in the group to shoot each bandit from long distance. Brad Avery carried with him a new rifle intended to be very accurate at long distances.

The rifle, an Enfield series of long rifles was first manufactured in 1894. When the posse spotted the men Brad would shoot each one without having an open gun fight.

With Seth Bullock's pent-up rage he did not intend to take any prisoners. The men on the trail went along with Seth's plan as many of their wives were on the train and had their fine jewelry taken from them in a rather rough manner.

The third mistake the robbers made was to build a small fire to stay warm on the very cool night. An Indian scout riding out front of Seth's group first spotted the fire and rode back to tell the posse.

Without waiting until morning, the posse dismounted their horses and a few men, including the sharpshooter, Brad Avery, very quietly approached the three men huddled beside their fire. Brad carefully loaded his Enfield and with the assistance of a very good scope was able to knock off each man in succession.

The posse then rode into the camp and recovered the stolen gold and other valuables that had been taken from the train.

When one of the men on the posse asked Seth if they should take the time to bury the outlaws Seth was reported to have said, "Hell no the buzzards and wolves will take care of their remains. Besides we didn't bring along any shovels."

It would take another couple of months to capture the other train robbers. However, Ivan Hutchinson and a couple of his other companions escaped to Texas and formed the Ivan Hutchinson Gang. It was reported that Hutchinson was killed in an ambush by Texas Rangers at Round Rock, Texas.

Chapter 13

A Bundle of Joy for Frank and Virginia

After riding the long distance home from the Badlands, Seth Bullock immediately rode to the hospital in Belle Fourche to see how his friend from Chicago was recovering from the severe blow to the head given to him by one of the train robbers.

As Seth was walking toward his friend Travis's hospital room, who should be ambling down the hallway but Frank Hall. Frank was in an exceptionally lighthearted mood and immediately pulled out a cigar to give to Seth.

Frank enthusiastically announced in a very loud voice for all to hear, "I am the proud father of a beautiful little girl!"

Seth gave Frank a big hug and said, "Boy, I am very happy for you and Virginia. It seems the two of you have been married only a few months."

"Yep," said Frank, "We didn't waste any time in adding to the Hall Dynasty."

As Seth was worried about his friend, he told Frank that after checking on Travis he would come to Virginia's room to see the new baby for the first time.

Seth was delighted to see Travis sitting in a large chair beside an open window admiring the grounds of the new hospital. Seth proceeded to tell Travis the story of how they were able to track down three of the train robbers, but they were unable to catch the ring leader of the gang.

When Travis wanted to know what happened when they caught the three desperados, Seth said, "Travis, you really don't want to know, but take my word for it, justice was served."

After about twenty minutes of conversation with Travis, Seth stopped a nurse in the hallway and asked where he might find Virginia Hall and her new born little girl. After getting instructions, Seth quickly made his way to Virginia's room.

Frank was sitting beside the bed but quickly got up and offered Seth his chair. Seth agreed that their little girl was the cutest little baby that he had ever seen. Seth then asked, "What handle are you going to give this precious little one?"

Frank answered by stating, "Virginia thought the name should be Stella."

A rather prolonged description concerning the train robbery and the tracking of the outlaws was told to anyone who would listen to Seth's story. However, when

Uncle Roy and Button stepped into the room the conversation changed to a much different subject.

Frank bent down to listen to what Virginia was whispering. Frank laughed and said, "Yes, Virginia, Button is not just gaining weight. Uncle Roy told me that they also are going to have a baby."

Virginia unthinkingly said, "But Roy aren't you a little old to start a family, after all Button already has two fine boys?"

Roy took some offense to the remark by answering, "Heck, Button and I are not yet fifty years old."

Frank remarked, "Yep, but as I remember my dad told me your fiftieth birthday is only two weeks away and so when the baby comes you will be fifty!"

With that remark, Seth Bullock laughed and told the group he was tired after the long posse ride and besides he did not want to be drawn into a family dispute. Anyway, Frank was very happy for Uncle Roy and Button and told his uncle that another young man would be welcome around the ranch. Virginia, admonished the two men and stated, "What makes you think that Button's baby will be a boy?"

Frank responded by saying that Button's other two children were boys so it was just natural that the third would be a boy. It was then that Virginia had to explain the facts of life to the two men by asking if their prize cattle always had bulls. Uncle Roy then says, "Well, Virginia, I guess you do have a good point, but we can only hope. Besides, I will need some young man to help on the ranch as I get a little older."

Frank was just jesting with his uncle when he said, "Uncle Roy, you already can take to the rocking chair on the front porch."

The two men continued to banter back and forth until the nurse stepped into the room and told the men to leave. It was feeding time for young Stella.

Frank asked Uncle Roy who was looking after the cattle on their ranch while he and Button were in Belle Fourche. To which Roy replied that Button's two boys, John and Harry took turns looking after Roy and Button's livestock.

Button was proud of her boys' independence in establishing their own ranches. In addition, she was very happy that the boys found Roy to be a real father figure and that the three men had gotten along so well.

As Roy had ridden his horse Silver into town, he asked if Button would mind riding alone back to the ranch in the buggy. Always an independent lady, Button agreed with one stipulation in that Roy load the buggy with the needed supplies from the general store. When she returned to the ranch both boys were there to greet their mother. Both John and Harry helped in unloading and putting away the supplies.

Roy wanted to check on a few of the cattle that had strayed too many miles from the main ranch. This effort would cost him much of the afternoon.

It was a good idea that Roy had checked on his herd as a few of the calves had been separated from the main group of cattle. It had been a long spell since there had been any disappearance of cattle due to rustlers.

However, a separated calf would be good prey for coyotes.

After locating the stray calves and bringing them back to the main herd, Roy quickly made his way back home.

John and Harry helped their mother with the chores and were invited to stay for supper. It was late when Roy made it back to the ranch. However, Button warmed up what was left of their supper and Roy seemed happy to finish off the meatloaf and mashed potatoes.

For a surprise Sarah had baked a fresh peach pie for Roy and her two boys.

Quickly, John excused himself from the table and made his way to the storm cellar. Without much light from the open door, John could not see the five foot "rattler" above the door.

The Author

Chapter 14

The Introduction of Barbed Wire on the Ranches

Although there had been conflicts about using barbed wire in Texas because this limited the cattlemen from driving their herds north, the ranchers in northwest South Dakota really did not have any difficulty with neighbors fencing in their property.

Many of the ranch owners in South Dakota had their property surveyed, and each knew the boundaries where their land ended and their neighbors' land began.

Therefore, to keep the herds of cattle from wandering too far from the main grazing areas each rancher started to place barbed wire around the boundaries of his property.

The one limitation was that it was against the law to stretch barbed wire across any public domain. This law was implemented in 1885.

Prior to the introduction of barbed wire, the cattle-men used Osage orange, a thorny bush which was time consuming to transplant and grow. The Osage orange later became a supplier of wood used in making barbed wire fence posts.

All of the ranchers were now busy stretching barbed wire around their pastureland. This would keep Roy and Button's boys busy for most of the summer. Also, the ranchers grew hay or wild grass to cut and store in the fields and barns to use as feed in the approaching long winters.

Since John and Harry volunteered to help Roy in stretching barbed wire around his property, Roy would assist each boy when he needed help on his ranch.

While the three men worked together on Roy and Button's ranch the boys' mother would have them stay for lunch.

That summer Button's healthy baby boy was born. They named him Everett.

Several months after the baby's birth John and Harry were at their parents' home for lunch when Button asked one of the boys to bring some bacon from the storm cellar.

Quickly, John excused himself from the table and made his way to the storm cellar. Without much light from the open cellar door, John could not see the five-foot rattlesnake above the door. The snake dropped down on John and bit him on his left hand.

With a yell, John hurried back to the house to tell what had just happened. Quickly, his brother Harry took Roy's rifle to the storm cellar and shot the rattler.

Roy had John lie down on the living room sofa and proceeded to cut John's left hand across the fang marks. Then Roy sucked out as mush poison as possible. The cut was probably deeper than it needed to be, and John would always have a long scar on his left hand.

After shooting the rattler Harry quickly hitched the horse to the buggy and Button and Roy raced to the doctor in Faith with John lying in the back of the buggy. Of course, their baby could not be left alone, so Button cuddled the little one in her arms as Roy handled the buggy reins.

The doctors in those early days did not have access to any anti-venom medicine, so many pioneers died from snakebite. But John was saved by the quick thinking of his step-father. Not only did he cut where the fang marks were, but also placed a tourniquet on John's upper arm to prevent the venom from proceeding to his upper body.

The doctor suggested that John stay in town that day and night just to be sure that he would be all right.

When Button and Roy returned to the ranch, Harry said in jest, "It was just like my older brother to be careless so that he would get out of helping Roy and me put up the fencing."

At first Button was upset by Harry's remark, but realized that her son was only kidding as she knew how close the boys were and Harry cared a lot about his older brother.

For the next week, Roy and Harry continued to dig holes to place the fence posts and then to string the barbed wire from post to post. This work was very exhausting and this particular summer was unusually hot on the barren prairie.

Often Button would know on which part of the ranch the men were working. If so, she took the buggy out to where they were located to take them their lunch and cold lemonade. John and baby Everett would ride along in the buggy when they went to the field. Lemonade was somewhat of an extravagance as lemons had to be imported, and they were expensive.

The men drove their working ranch wagon to hold the wire and posts. They also had a trusty rifle with them in case they spotted a rattler or coyote. They would also shoot prairie dogs. The holes the dogs dug in the rangeland were dangerous as horses would often step in them and break their legs.

After a few weeks of building fences, it was time for the men to cut the hay and gather the feed. The feed needed to be closer to where the cattle would spend their long winters.

When the work on Roy's ranch was complete, Roy helped both John and Harry cut hay on their ranches. As John was still recovering from his snake bite, a drifter by the name of Mark was hired to complete the cutting and move the hay closer to the homestead.

Chapter 15

Tex Bennett and the Texas Rangers

Meanwhile, back in his home state Tex Bennett had distanced himself from the unsavory characters who had hired him in Paris, Texas. Once belonging to the "Texas Regulars," Tex had not participated in the killing of Mr. Champion and had evaded capture by the 6th Cavalry that had ridden to the rescue of the "Regulars."

As Paris, Texas, is north and west of Dallas on the Oklahoma border, Tex thought it would be a good idea for him to relocate far enough away so that no one could associate him with the "Regulars."

One early morning, Tex saddled his trusty horse and rode south and west. After several days he settled in San Antonio. Being short on cash and with cattlemen not hiring wranglers, Tex decided to once again be on the "right side of the law" and joined the Texas Rangers.

Although the enforcement agency was based in Austin, Texas, the Rangers had an office in San Antonio. Tex knew that during the Rangers' long history the men had settled many a dispute and apprehended many an outlaw.

The captain of the Rangers asked Tex if he had been in any outlaw activities. Of course, Tex would answer "no" to the question, hoping that there would be no follow-up to his past history.

Many Rangers were enlisted to fight for the Confederacy following the secession of Texas from the United States in 1861 during the American Civil War. Tex was too young to have witnessed this period of history.

Caption Grover of the Rangers needed to hire as many men as possible, as the Mexican Revolution beginning in 1910 had spilled over into Texas. The Mexican peasants were fighting against President Diaz.

Without Federal Cavalry in the area, the breakdown of law and order on the Mexican side of the border meant the Rangers were once again called upon to restore and maintain law and order.

Luckily for Tex, the need for new Rangers meant that hundreds of new special Rangers were hired without the careful screening given most of the new recruits.

In 1918, a massacre of at least 15 Mexican men and boys ranging in age from 16 to 72 years in the tiny border town of Porvenir, Texas, in western Presidio County brought dozens of Rangers to the location.

History will relate that before the decade was over, thousands of lives were lost, Texans and Mexicans alike. In January 1919, an investigation by the Texas Legislature found that from 300 to 5,000 people, mostly Hispanics, had been killed by Rangers from 1910 to 1919. Also, many acts of brutality and injustice were reported to have been carried out by the Rangers.

Although Tex would not reveal what his activities were during his service with the Rangers, it was discovered that a few Ranger companies were responsible for confining and removing Indians by tightly controlling the mixed blood people.

The Rangers were also accused of assisting the large-scale ranchers against the small-scale ranchers and farmers who fenced the land. They also helped break the power of labor unions that tried to organize the workers, both in the agricultural fields and industrial corporations.

Tex had always had a conscience and thought that although the Rangers were primarily good and honest men, some of their orders just did not seem justified. Therefore, after a couple of years he sought other means of support.

Luck would have it that a large Texas ranch on the border with Mexico had hired a few wranglers and were advertising for more cowboys. As Tex had worked with large herds of cattle, he thought this would be a good place for him to go.

The owner of the large spread was John H. Hardin. Now, Mr. Hardin had married a Mexican by the name of Rose Rodrigues. Their daughter was a tall beautiful girl about the same age as Tex.

Immediately, the two became enamored with each other and both made every attempt possible to see each other. Of course, with the strict Mexican morals, the two always had a chaperon when they courted.

After a few months of seeing each other on a regular basis, Tex asked to speak with Mr. Hardin. After a long conversation with Mr. Hardin who wanted to know every detail of Tex's life – including his parents, the blessing was finally given for the two to marry.

A short time after the wedding Mr. Hardin decided to thin his herd and enjoy retirement. He sold the ranch and gave permission for Tex and Maria to travel to South Dakota where Tex was offered the job as foreman of Frank and Virginia's vast ranch lands.

At first Maria was wary of leaving her family, but after much persuasion by Tex, Maria agreed to the move as now Tex would have a steady job and perhaps a bright future with his old friend Frank Hall.

Chapter 16

The Cavalry at Fort Meade

Frank Hall continued to add livestock to his vastly increasing herd as he now had plenty of good pasture land for his cattle to graze on. He had even hired a couple of wranglers to assist in the development of his holdings.

Taking a lesson from Seth Bullock, it was time to look for other opportunities to increase his wealth. One evening while talking with Virginia, Frank had the idea of selling good horses to the Cavalry post at Fort Meade, near Sturgis, South Dakota.

Fort Meade was established in 1878 to protect the new settlements in the northern Black Hills, especially the nearby gold mining area around Deadwood.

Several stage and freight routes passed through Fort Meade to Deadwood. After the disaster of the 7th Cavalry at the Battle of the Little Big Horn, the troopers were stationed at the Fort.

Fort Meade had been built to accommodate a regiment of at least ten full cavalry troops and it was now regarded as a very strategic post in the West. The War Department still thought that the Indians in that part of the plains needed to be watched and kept on their reservations. There was still a lot of built-up hatred for what happened at the Battle of the Little Big Horn in Montana.

One bright morning, in early spring, Frank told Virginia that he was going to meet with the post commander at Fort Meade in an attempt to establish good relations and perhaps convince the Colonel to buy horses from the Halls.

The post commander, Colonel C.H. Carleton had served as the commander of Fort Meade since January of 1891. When Frank entered his office, the Colonel rose to greet Frank and asked him to sit in the large leather overstuffed chair beside his desk. Together they discussed the weather and mundane events while enjoying coffee in the Colonel's spacious office.

Colonel Carleton was every bit a true "horse soldier" with a ramrod stature. Although only about five feet seven inches tall, the Colonel had the respect of his men and enforced the strict regulations of all cavalry posts in the West. The Colonel's uniform had been starched and every insignia was in its proper place on his military shirt. Frank also noted several combat ribbons.

After Frank gave the Colonel the reason for his visit, the Colonel stated, "Mr. Hall, we have very strict standards for the horses we buy for our troopers. They must all be at least sixteen hands high and be either chestnut or black. In fact, I am thinking about establishing a group of our very finest troopers to participate in ceremonies that are held in the local towns in the Black Hills." The Colonel continued by stating that he wanted all of the horses to be dark black without any distinguishing markings so they all looked alike.

The plan must have been on the Colonel's mind for some time, as he had already requisitioned brand new uniforms and selected the troopers to form this parade-ready unit.

After leaving Colonel Carleton's office, Frank felt confident that he could make the sale if he could just get the right horses. He decided to have his ranch foreman Tex ride down to Texas and purchase some horses which would meet the Colonel's standards. If the horses were not acceptable, Tex could move on up to Kentucky and select the horses from the Blue Grass state.

Arriving back at the ranch Frank summoned Tex to the ranch house to explain what was needed to fulfill the possible contract with Colonel Carleton. He also told Tex not to worry if the horses were not completely saddle-broken, as the wranglers on the ranch would have them parade ground ready in time for the big parade.

It took Tex and a couple of wranglers a few weeks to ride from the Hall ranch into Texas. Tex did not find any horses there that would meet the standards set by the Army and so moved on to Kentucky.

One evening, at about dusk, Stella glanced out the window and spotted a large dust cloud in the distance. "Dad, we either have a herd of buffalo heading our way or someone is driving either cattle or horses onto our ranch," she shouted.

Frank immediately saddled his horse and headed out to what was Tex's herd of horses that he had driven all the way from Kentucky. Frank, after dismounting and looking over the fine stock of thirty horses, shook Tex's hand and said, "You really know your horses. These studs are the best group of horses in this part of the country, and the Colonel should be very pleased."

Virginia and Stella walked out to the group and greeted Tex and the two wranglers. While Virginia was admiring the fine animals, Stella, nearing her teenage years, was more interested in what the two wranglers looked like.

Virginia, being wise in the ways of the West, stated, "Now the real work begins as we must break these horses in only about six weeks and have them accepted by Colonel Carleton."

Frank, Virginia, Stella and the three cowboys enjoyed a good meal that both Virginia and Stella had put together. As Tex and the wranglers had been on the trail for several weeks, they heartedly enjoyed the meal of steak, mashed potatoes, fresh beans and all the fixings. After the main course the men had a choice of either peach or apple pie – or a slice of both.

Following the very fine meal, the men moved to the living room to discuss the work that was ahead of them in order to meet the Colonel's deadline. During this time, Tex leaned next to Frank and stated, "I notice that you and Virginia are expecting another cowhand to add to your family."

"Yep," says Frank, "Virginia is expecting and we should have a fine young bouncing boy by this fall."

Whereas, one of the wranglers laughed and said, "Mr. Hall, how do you know this will be a boy?"

Frank answered by saying, "Because I need to keep the Hall name on the ranch." The topic was not pursued any further that evening. However, less than two weeks later Virginia had a bad fall in the barn, broke her left wrist and had a miscarriage. This was to be her last pregnancy.

To everyone's surprise who should ride up to the ranch the next morning but Uncle Roy and Stella's younger brother Marion. Tex had been with the Rangers for several years now and was behind on Hall family happenings. Even though Tex had been working with Frank for several months now, Frank had forgotten to mention that about a year after Stella was born the young Marion had been conceived. Now being about twelve years old, Marion looked very much like his father Frank and had the same mannerisms. Marion enjoyed spending time with his Uncle Roy when he was not in school.

Frank had built a very sturdy corral to keep the thirty horses in. One by one a Texas wrangler would attempt to "break" each horse so that they would tolerate a saddle and a man. All three of the cowboys had the ability to calm each horse without resorting to whipping or in any way harming the horses. The technique was known as "horse whispering."

Each morning, after Stella prepared a large breakfast of eggs, bacon and bread soaked in the bacon fat, the cowboys would begin their long day working with the horses. Virginia tried to help with food preparation and other house chores as much as she could with her wrist in a cast and still recovering from the miscarriage. Frank had hired a young girl from a neighboring ranch to help in the house until Virginia completely recovered from her fall.

Stella would sit on the fence posts and watch each wrangler work with the horses. Frank had taught Stella to ride, and she was very good working and being around livestock. Of course, prior to Stella's visit to the corral, she would need to complete all chores assigned by her mother. This would mean helping in baking bread and those wonderful pies that the cowboys thought were so delicious.

Virginia and Frank noticed that Stella was spending more time pampering herself in her bedroom before appearing for breakfast. Stella found one wrangler by the name of Otto to be quite handsome and would purposely attempt conversations and ask about his state of Texas. Otto was tall with coal black hair and displayed a cool confidence that many a young lady would find attractive.

The process of breaking the horses took almost the entire summer before Frank sent one of his ranch hands to summon Colonel Carleton to the ranch to view the new stock of horses.

Colonel Carleton, along with his first sergeant and four other troopers, arrived at Frank's ranch about mid-morning on one fine September day. The Colonel rode very tall in the saddle and sat on a beautiful horse with full-flowing mane.

After thorough examination of each horse, the Colonel and his first sergeant walked to the far corner of the corral to discuss how many and which horses they would buy.

Frank invited the Colonel and first sergeant to come to the house to draw up some papers. Of course, Virginia was included in the conversation as she had a very good understanding of the worth of horses. She actually controlled the bookkeeping and cash flow of the expanding holdings of the Hall family.

Frank was somewhat disappointed in that the Colonel selected only twenty of the thirty horses that Tex had brought from Kentucky. However, both Frank and Virginia were surprised at how much each horse was worth to the Cavalry.

For payment Frank gave Tex and each of the wranglers one horse and the agreed upon cash as part of their pay for the many weeks they had worked on the ranch and the time spent on the trail.

All the men agreed on one condition. The condition was that each could select the horse he would receive as payment. Frank agreed with this arrangement. He still had seven horses to attempt to sell in the local market.

Frank and his son Marion rode into Belle Fourche with the seven horses and placed them in the town's auction barn. Each Wednesday the town had a sale of both cattle and horses. To no one's surprise Seth Bullock bought all seven horses.

Seth had a good eye for quality horses, and the new stock from Kentucky was an exceptionally good buy for that part of the plains.

In payment for the twenty horses that were sold to Colonel Carleton, it was standard practiced to hand Frank a formal document disclosing the number of horses bought and the price of each horse.

Now the problem was for Frank to redeem the check at the military post at Fort Leavenworth, Kansas. Frank wanted to obtain the total amount paid by the Army, as he needed to purchase feed and other staples prior to the anticipated long winter that would be approaching in a couple of months.

Chapter 17

Attempted Robbery

Colonel Carleton brought several troupers with him to decide on which horses to buy from Frank Hall. One of the troupers had been in trouble with the law prior to joining the Army.

Trooper Carl had witnessed the transfer of the pay document to Mr. Hall. The trooper thought about contacting his friends on the "outside" to stage a robbery on the messenger whom Frank Hall would send to Fort Leavenworth to collect the horse payment.

During the entire ride back to Fort Meade from the Hall ranch, Trooper Carl was lost in thought on just how to get word to his friends and when to attack Mr. Hall's courier after he collected the money from the central headquarters at Fort Leavenworth.

Finally, Carl had a plan. Since he was owed a few days' leave, he would telegraph his unsavory friends and meet them in Deadwood. It was ironic that the men would meet in Saloon Number 10 – the location where "Wild Bill" Hickok was killed.

It was decided that Trooper Carl would notify his three friends with a description of the courier and when he would leave for Kansas. The idea was for the courier to be ambushed on the trail back to the Hall ranch.

Frank decided to send his most trustworthy wrangler to Fort Leavenworth to bring back the money earned by the sale of the horses. Ruben had now worked on the Hall ranch for a couple of years and was a local boy from a very religious family. Frank thought that there would not be a better man than Ruben to carry out this assignment.

Arriving early in Fort Leavenworth, the three co-conspirators waited just outside the Fort and after a couple of days viewed a ranch hand slowly riding his mount to the gates of the Fort and then entering.

After finishing a meal in the mess hall, Ruben immediately made his way to post headquarters with the necessary document to collect the Halls' money.

Ruben thought about his ride back to the Hall ranch and the danger he might be in if any strangers knew what he was carrying. Therefore, prior to leaving the Fort, Ruben made a purchase of a large carpetbag. Ruben had planned to place the cash in the large bag and securely tie the bag to the back of his saddle.

Instead, in Ruben's private barracks room the carpetbag was carefully loaded and bundled with cut up newspapers.

Ruben was wise beyond his years. He had requested that the vast majority of the money owed the Halls would consist of a money order that would be made out to Frank Hall. The money order would be placed in a leather pouch that would ride under the saddle blanket on his way back to the Hall ranch.

Leaving prior to sunup, Ruben purposely did not ride back the same route he had taken into Kansas. However, Trooper Carl's friends quickly picked up Ruben's trail and followed him the remainder of the day.

The ride back to South Dakota took a few days. The outlaws thought that the best time to rob the Hall courier would be in the middle of the night. However, during the last night on the trail the desperados thought they heard the courier digging in the ground just outside his well-lit campfire. The outlaws thought Ruben was burying the stash and would return for the money when he thought he was no longer being followed. The outlaws even witnessed Ruben rolling small boulders to place on top of the newly dug hole.

Although the desperados thought they had been careful in staying well behind the Hall courier, this cowboy messenger must have detected that he was being followed.

Now the plan changed and instead of robbing the young courier in the night, they would wait until the Hall cowboy departed the campsite in the morning and then they would ride in and dig up the cash.

The next morning, after Ruben disappeared over the first hill, he put a whip to his horse to gain distance between himself and Trooper Carl's accomplices.

Trooper Carl's fellow desperados were busy that morning moving the boulders and then digging into the loosely piled dirt. Buried about two feet down was the carpetbag. Eagerly, the men tore open the bag to find only cut up newspapers.

By this time Ruben was approaching the Hall property. He stopped at a neighbor's ranch to explain that he was probably being followed and asked a couple of their ranch hands to bring their rifles with them and ride on with him to the Hall ranch. Of course, the rancher released his best two wranglers to accompany Ruben back home.

Riding hard the would-be robbers now witnessed the courier with two well-armed escorts and broke off the chase.

Frank hurried outside to greet Rubin and was dismayed that what appeared to be his trusted employee without the carpetbag full of his money.

Ruben laughed at Frank's concern and then dismounted and carefully reached under his saddle blanket and produced the leather pouch with the bank draft. Ruben stated to Frank, "Mr. Hall, I think that Mr. Bullock's bank in Belle Fourche will cash this for you."

Frank slapped Ruben on the back and exclaimed that he was the smartest cowhand he had ever employed. Furthermore, as a reward Frank gave Ruben a $20 bill for his time and the risk he had endured.

It was only a couple of weeks after Ruben had returned to the Hall ranch that a trooper arrived at the ranch with a dispatch sent by none other than the commanding officer, Colonel Carleton. His dispatch was a formal invitation to the upcoming ceremony at Fort Meade. The elite horse troop had practiced its parade drill and was ready to display the fine-tuned precision drill while mounted. Even the post's military band had practiced and was ready to give the locals in the area a very fine performance.

All of the horse troopers would form a parade on the grounds with the band leading the way. Immediately behind the band would be a horse led by the first sergeant. The horse was Comanche, the only survivor of the 7th Cavalry Battle of the Little Big Horn led by Custer in Montana.

To a surprise to no one at the drill, Colonel Caleb H. Carleton, 8th Cavalry, had all the guests rise as the post band played *The Star Spangled Banner*. It was at this lonely cavalry outpost on the western frontier that *The Star Spangled Banner* first became the official music for the military retreat ceremony. The playing of this particular music happened long before the arrangement became the National Anthem.

On the buggy ride home it was Frank's son Marion who said to his father, "Dad, I would one day like to join the cavalry and become a trooper." Frank Hall ignored his son's statement as it was Frank's plan to have his son take over the ranch as his holdings continued to expand.

Everything would have worked out fine for Poker Alice if an unfortunate incident had not happened in 1913.

The Author

Chapter 18

Poker Alice's Casino and Brothel

Colonel Carleton really did not have any discipline problems on his tour of duty at Fort Meade as he followed a very strict Code of Conduct. He also expected his men to always be respectful and obey both the military and civilian laws. This is perhaps because he was a devout Methodist and neither smoked or drank alcohol.

When Alice Ivers opened a brothel and gambling casino just a few miles from the post, the Colonel was visibly upset and held a conference with his senior officers to find out if there was any military or civilian law that could close this establishment.

After the Colonel read numerous military articles and contacted Washington, it became apparent that from a military point of view nothing could be done to close this "Den of Depravity."

After operating a gaming house in Deadwood for a number of years, Alice met and married Warren G. Tubbs. Tubbs was also a card player but had little of the skill of Alive Ivers. Therefore, Tubbs had a second job as housepainter in Sturgis, South Dakota.

The romance between Tubbs and Ivers was said to have started when Alice shot a man in the arm who had been threatening Tubbs with a knife. She and Tubbs married and had seven children.

In Deadwood Alive was reported to have made as much as $6,000 playing poker during one extended evening. This was a considerable amount of money in those days.

As Tubbs lost more money when he gambled than he won, it was Alive who would stake Tubbs for gambling money so that he could continue playing.

After living in Deadwood for many years, Tubbs persuaded Alice to move to his ranch. He lived only a short period of time at the ranch before contracting pneumonia. Alice liked the peace and quiet of the ranch but needed money to pay her ever mounting bills. After Tubbs died Alice used the family horse-drawn wagon to take his body back to Sturgis for burial.

Alice then hired George Huckert to take care of the ranch while she returned to Sturgis to earn some money to pay her back debts. Finally, Huckert proposed and Alice married him in Sturgis.

The marriage did not last long as Huckert died in 1913. Alice continued to call herself Alice Tubbs.

About 1910 Alice had purchased an old house on Bear Butte Creek near the Fort Mead Army Post. Alice thought that in addition to gambling she could make big money by also running a brothel.

As the small house had needed extra work she had borrowed money and added rooms to the building. She then made a train trip to Kansas City to recruit a few "girls."

When Alice repaid the loan in less than two years, the banker asked how she was able to recoup the money so rapidly. She was reported to have said, "Well it's this way. I knew the Grand Army of the Republic was having an encampment here in Sturgis. And I knew that the state Elks convention would be here too. But I plumb forgot about all those Methodist preachers coming to town for a conference."

Everything would have worked out fine for Poker Alice if an unfortunate incident had not happened in about 1913. It seems that a number of soldiers from Fort Meade came into the establishment and became unruly.

Poker Alice fired a single rifle shot to quiet the horse soldiers. However, the bullet ripped into two of them, killing one. When the local sheriff arrived, he took Alice and her six "ladies" to jail. In the process, they shut down the brothel. Alice was later acquitted of any wrongdoing because the soldiers were in a near riot. Anyway, the shooting was deemed an accident.

But Colonel Carleton wanted to permanently close the "gentlemen's club." Finally, Poker Alice agreed to close her establishment after being arrested several times for running a brothel. Alice was sentenced to the state penitentiary but as she was by this time 75 years old, the governor pardoned her and she was then in permanent retirement.

Needless to say, Colonel Carleton was overjoyed to see the end of this problem. From the time they closed Poker Alice's brothel until Colonel Carleton retired he was very satisfied with his job and accomplishments at Fort Meade.

Chapter 19

Economic Development

With the population of Belle Fourche and the surrounding area rapidly expanding, it was Seth Bullock and his business partners who contributed greatly to the improvement of the entire area.

In 1916 Seth Bullock sold enough land to the Great Western Sugar Company so that they were able to raise sugar beets. The company representative visited Seth Bullock's home and told Mr. Bullock that they needed a minimum of 8,000 acres in order to support growing sugar beets. It would take another ten years before operations would begin in raising and then processing the sugar beets.

This was no problem to Bullock and his partners as they could offer twice that amount of acreage. One problem that had to be dealt with was that harvesting the beets was very labor intensive and not many families in the area surrounding Belle Fourche would accept work on the sugar beet farms.

Therefore, the labor for both planting and harvesting the beets would mean importing Mexicans, as they would accept this back-breaking work and demand little in compensation. The Mexicans were happy to have the opportunity to earn American dollars and could take their wages back to Mexico.

Seth Bullock introduced the raising of alfalfa on his huge ranch. Alfalfa was a good source of feed for the many cattle that now populated the entire western South Dakota plains.

The Belle Fourche area tripled in population in the years between 1900 and 1910. One reason was that this was a transportation hub used for cattlemen to send their livestock to Chicago and Omaha.

Also, about this time the first major federal irrigation projects were started near Belle Fourche with the building of Orman Dam. When it was completed in 1910, it was reported to be the world's largest earth-filled dam. With available water for irrigation, many crops were able to flourish in the area. Crops that were once raised only in the Midwestern states were now available. In addition to sugar beets the area could now support such crops as corn, hay and even cucumbers.

History will support the fact that sugar beets were raised well into the late 1950's and early 1960's.

The Swango and Hall families decided to continue raising cattle, even though there were now a few sheep introduced to the plains.

John Swango was reported to have said, "Those damn sheep ruin good pasture land as they pull the grass from the roots and leave good grazing land a long time to recover." There continued to be some unrest between the cattlemen and sheep growers. But unlike other parts of the country, there never was an outright war between the two groups.

The cordial relations between the sheepmen and the cattlemen did not extend to all regions of the western states. There were wars between the two groups in Texas, Arizona and the border region of Wyoming and Colorado.

Generally, the cattlemen saw the sheepherders as invaders who destroyed the public grazing lands which they had to share on a first-come, first-served basis.

It has been reported that between 1870 and 1920, approximately 120 skirmishes occurred in eight different states and territories. At least fifty-four men were killed and some 50,000 to over 100,000 sheep were slaughtered.

Both the Hall and Swango families were not going to get involved in any dispute as the primary problem was on the Wyoming and Colorado border. However, Button's oldest son John had left home and now was working on a Colorado cattle ranch in the northern part of the state.

A letter home from John stated that the owner of the cattle ranch he worked for was organizing a group of men to stop the sheepherders from crossing into Colorado.

John wanted his family to know that he was not involved in any gunfight, as he had been assigned a job of rounding up stray cattle that had wandered south away from the Wyoming border.

Abraham Wilkes, the owner of the large cattle ranch had not sent for John to help in a possible dispute. Mr. Wilkes thought he had enough guns to stop those "damn smelly" sheepmen from crossing into his range land in Colorado.

It was in Routt County that the major conflict occurred. The cattlemen attempted to keep the Wyoming sheepherders from entering their grazing ranges.

The *Cheyenne Reader* reported that, "Cowboys were sent out to scour the country and warn the settlers that sheepmen now holding their flocks on Snake River at the Wyoming border were contemplating an invasion of the Bear River cattle ranges. The effect was electrical, and by noon today 350 cattlemen and feeders were assembled to decide upon positive action to keep the sheep back . . ."

It was this show of force whereby the cattlemen adopted a series of resolutions that established dead-lines and effectively banned all sheepherders from entering northwestern Colorado.

To further scare the sheepmen from attempting to run their sheep into Colorado, the *Cheyenne Reader* again warned of the cattlemen putting together a force of eight hundred to a thousand gunmen to enforce their regulations.

As a result of the warning from the newspaper in Cheyenne, the sheepherders respected the cattlemen's resolve which diffused the situation before it became too serious.

There were still reports of cattlemen crossing the border and killing thousands of sheep. On one such invasion, over 3,000 sheep were "clubbed and scattered." The shepherds were robbed and their wagons were burned.

Due to a decline of open rangeland and changes in ranching practices, most of the causes for hostilities ended.

To occupy their time the next generation of the Halls soon developed an interest in competing in the local rodeos in the area. It seemed that every town in the Black Hills of South Dakota had its own rodeo.

The Author

Chapter 20

The Later Years

Now that Frank and Virginia had two children in their teenage years, it was Uncle Roy's turn to add to his family with a strapping young boy. Button and Roy now had one child of their own whom they called Everett.

The Spanish-American war had concluded with only Button's oldest son John having served in Cuba. John witnessed very little combat and soon returned to the ranch. All family members seemed destined to carry on their very successful lives raising the very best Herefords in Western South Dakota.

As was the practice in past years, all of the ranchers thinned their herds in the fall by sending them by rail to markets in either Chicago or Omaha. The farmers in eastern South Dakota and Iowa had much better soil to raise corn that was used to feed the cattle prior to sending the cattle to market.

To occupy their spare time, the next generation of the Halls soon developed an interest in competing in the local rodeos in the area. It seemed that every town in the Black Hills of South Dakota had its own rodeo.

In the East the states had county fairs. Both county fairs and local rodeos were very similar, but each had its own particular activities that differed.

As you will remember, Uncle Roy was very good with his lariat, and taught Button's boys how to use the lasso. All of the wranglers on a cattle ranch had to be good using their lariat as in the spring the newborn calves needed to be branded.

Both John and Harry had practiced and had developed great skill with their lariats. Consequently, Roy urged them to enter the local rodeo's calf roping contests. With the encouragement of their step-father both boys entered numerous contests and always seemed to bring home ribbons – not always the blue ribbon. Nevertheless, they were in the top three of the competition.

Frank and Virginia's daughter, Stella, was a very pretty young girl who was now in her early twenties and entered and won many beauty contests. She had also attended college for a couple of years and now Frank and Virginia had turned over to her the bookkeeping of their vast holdings.

However, Stella's younger brother Marion was a rough and tough cowhand who "broke" many a saddle horse for the Hall's neighbors. Therefore, Marion entered contests in both saddle and bare-back riding.

Marion's parents would not let him enter the bull riding contests as they thought this a little too dangerous. Marion argued with his parents to let him try to ride a bull. However, Frank absolutely forbid his entering these contests as he told Marion that he needed help on the ranch and a cowhand with a broken arm or leg would not be very much help. Of course, there was always the possibility of being gored by the bull.

Tex was now the foreman on Frank and Virginia's ranch. He and his wife had two boys of their own. The Bennett boys were Leslie and Casey. They were both in their mid-teens and so proved to be helpful around the ranch.

Tex's wife, Maria was a tall beauty with long black hair. When she assisted on the ranch, she would place her hair in long braids. With her olive complexion she often was mistaken as an Indian.

Unfortunately, the settlers in this part of the state still harbored some bad feelings toward Indians. But with Maria's sweet personality, she would win over the hearts of the neighbors. Maria was always helping other neighbors and had established a true friendship with all the ranchers' wives.

The years passed quickly for the Hall and Swango families. They were hard workers, and their good health and energy allowed them to acquire more and more land and the respect of their neighbors.

After a brief illness, with what some suspect as cancer, Frank's father passed away in 1900 and his mother succumbed to heart failure in 1902. Don and Mary Ann's holdings were then passed on to Frank.

The Swangos died together in an auto accident in 1918. It seemed that John had drifted off the road with their car landing in a stock pond beside the road. Neither John nor his wife Ellen was able to escape the rushing water as it filled the car.

Chapter 21

Stella's Romance

With Stella's very sharp financial knowledge, she supervised the business operation of the Hall families. In addition to the ever increasing number of the very best registered Hereford cattle, the family money was invested in a host of other operations.

It was fortuitous that Stella had met Eric Anderson the operations manager of the Great Western Sugar Company during a social gathering on Christmas Eve of 1926. From Stella's business sources she was able to discern that the company would begin operations in the Belle Fourche area in the near future.

With the information gleaned that evening, Stella immediately began to purchase the type of ground best suited to the growing of sugar beets. The land was in addition to what Seth Bullock had purchased in 1916.

Many in town, including the local banker, thought that Stella was paying way too much for the land she acquired.

However, Eric Anderson had given Stella enough information about the company that she knew this to be a good investment.

Eric was immediately smitten by Stella's beauty and charm. However, it took Stella a few months to see that, in fact, Eric was a better looking man than those she had been dating in the area. Furthermore, as she was approaching thirty-five years of age, she thought this was the best available prospect for marriage. Sometimes, Stella would let her head overrule her emotions.

With additional dating, the two became quite intimate and to no one's surprise Stella announced to her brother and Uncle Roy that she was now engaged to Eric Anderson.

Neither Eric nor Stella planned to have a big wedding. Rather, only the immediate family would gather in the Methodist Church in Belle Fourche for a traditional wedding. They had simple organ music and one soloist.

Now that travel was much more accessible, the two spent their honeymoon in Denver, Colorado. Instead of the buggy that Stella's parents rode into Belle Fourche for their honeymoon, Stella and Eric had their own new Lincoln.

While in Colorado the two had time to explore the area and together decided that the land around Greeley, Colorado, showed great possibilities. Many ranchers were ready to sell their land and move on to other regions of the country.

With their combined capital, Eric and Stella purchased several hundred acres of land. The expansion to other regions of the country was now in full operation.

Upon returning to the Belle Fourche area, the two newlyweds purchased a very fine mansion that was now on the market. The previous owners had reached that age when they were forced to move in with their children. The older couple's health continued to decline, and they lived only a few months with their oldest daughter before passing on.

It seemed to be only a few weeks later that Stella and Eric announced that they would become parents in a few months. When questioned by Stella's brother Marion when the baby would be born, Stella, turning red in the face, told her younger brother, "Just you never mind, that is Eric's and my business and you will know in due time."

The announcement was made at the traditional Sunday noon meal in Stella and Eric's mansion. Marion had brought his girlfriend, Charlene, to dinner that particular day. He pushed his chair away from the table, stood up, raised his class of champagne, and clinked his fork against the glass to get everyone's attention.

"Well, not to be outdone by my big sister, I too have an announcement to make. Charlene and I are going to be married. She has accepted my proposal." With this announcement, the thought of Stella having a baby so soon after the wedding was forgotten in the congratulatory hugs given by all at the dinner table.

After an elaborate wedding, held at the Bullock Hotel in Belle Fourche, Marion and Charlene decided to honeymoon in Denver, just as Marion's big sister had done.

The destination was not a whim by Marion. He wanted to view the land holdings that Stella had purchased near Greeley, Colorado. After viewing the lovely setting of Greeley and the outstanding growth of grass, Marion telegraphed his sister that indeed she and Eric had made a good investment.

Several months later, Eric and Stella announced the birth of their first born whom they named David. Everyone in the Hall family celebrated the new parents. This was the first grandchild in the family.

Marion and Charlene's first son James was born that next year. James was full of life and somewhat of a mischievous child. From the time he was walking, James enjoyed taking part in the necessary chores on the ranch. Eighteen months later Cole was born.

As James and Cole grew into manhood, they worked well with their father. Keeping track of their large herd and the family's acquisitions was an ever demanding job.

Chapter 22

The Hall Women

Several years after James and Cole were born; Charlene gave birth to a delicate baby girl whom they named Alice. This new child was cherished beyond belief since her parents were getting older and feared they would not have any more children.

From the beginning Alice was a difficult child. She was continuously fussy, didn't sleep at night and did not eat well. Marion and Charlene took her to the doctor regularly for checkups, but the doctor did not find anything seriously wrong. She was just a fussy child.

When Alice was about four months old, she developed a severe cold which led to pneumonia. After six days in the hospital in Spearfish the little girl died. What a shock! The entire Hall family was devastated. They had lost one of their own. Most of the older family members kept themselves isolated from their friends and neighbors to deal with their grief. The younger Halls continued doing their chores and going to school.

Eighteen months later Marion and Charlene were blessed with another baby girl who turned out to be their last child. This time they chose the name Eleanor.

Eleanor Hall was the complete opposite of her older sister. She was a happy child from the day she was brought home from the hospital and she remained healthy. She was honest, respectful and always smiling. When she started school, classmates considered her a leader. She took music lessons, learned to play the piano and sang in the school and church choirs.

Always independent, Eleanor learned to drive a car which she drove to high school in Spearfish and later to the local college in Spearfish.

Near the end of her first year in college, Eleanor met Dr. Sam Dawson who had just arrived in Spearfish to set up medical practice. They started dating and married the next fall.

Because of her husband's demanding profession, Eleanor agreed to leave the ranch and make her home in Spearfish. Eventually as their family grew, they built a large place where they remained for the rest of their lives.

Being the wife of a local doctor, Eleanor was expected to entertain regularly. This she did with the skill and confidence she had learned from her mother and grandmother.

During the next twelve years Eleanor and Dr. Sam had four children. The first pregnancy resulted in twins – Patrick and Donald. Next came Ella and Jane about three years apart.

Eleanor raised her four children and supported her husband in his growing medical practice. In addition, she became a civic leader in Spearfish, serving on many committees which helped the city to grow and prosper.

Timing is very important for winning the contest. From being motionless James must spur his horse into a full gallop to chase the calf. Therefore, the burst of the horse out of the chute is very important.

The Author

Chapter 23

The Rodeo Comes to Town

As the years passed and Stella's son David grew into manhood, he participated in the branding of the cattle in the spring and took a turn in breaking in new saddle horses for the wranglers on the ranch to ride.

As David was exposed to all of the western lore of the area, he soon became attached to first watching and then participating in the local rodeos. Much to his parents' objection, David found that he was very good in both saddle bronco and bareback bronco horse contests.

The horses used in the competition were specially bred for strength, agility, and bucking ability. Due to the rigors of travel between where the rodeos were being held and the short bursts of high intensity work required, most bucking horses were at least 6 or 7 years old.

The bucking horse was held in a wooden enclosure called a bucking chute. Each cowboy then climbed onto the penned horse. When the rider was ready by winding his hand around a rawhide strap, the gate of the bucking chute was opened and the horse burst out and began to buck.

The rider attempted to stay on the horse for a minimum of eight seconds without touching the horse with his free hand. On the first jump out of the chute the cowboy must "mark the horse out." This means he must have the heels of his boots – with spurs attached – contact the horse above the point of the shoulders before the horse's front legs hit the ground.

A rider who managed to complete a ride was scored on a scale of 0-50 and the horse was also scored on a scale of 0-50. This was the reason that David looked over the stock of bucking horses prior to the contest in hope of riding a horse that was mean enough to score in the forty or above category. Often David would talk with other contestants to find the horses that were better than others in the competition.

David hoped that on each ride he would achieve a total score of at least in the 80's.

Of course, the horse would also need to be mean enough to give a good ride. David wanted a horse that would buck in a spectacular and effective manner. If he drew a horse that bucked in a straight line with no significant changes of direction the score would be lower.

David's special saddle was equipped with free swinging stirrups and no horn. David would lift the reins and attempt to find a rhythm with the horse by spurring forwards and backwards with his feet.

When David competed in the bareback contests he would not use a saddle or rein, rather he placed one hand to grip a simple handle on a rigging placed on the horse just at the horse's withers.

David would then lean back against the bucking horse and spur up and down with his legs, again in rhythm with the motion of the horse.

David won many ribbons in the contests that he entered. However, although a couple of blue ribbons were won, it seemed that a cowboy by the name of Earl Bascom won more blue ribbons and the cash prizes that went along with the winning ride.

Being only a little over a year younger than David, Marion and Charlene's son James would also participate in the local rodeos. Now, James being somewhat smaller in statue than his cousin David did not welcome being bucked off horses and hitting the ground.

Rather, with the help of Uncle Roy's children, James soon became the winner of calf roping contests. James was quick in spurring his horse to quickly throw his rope around the calf's neck.

To explain how calf roping works, one needs to know that the calves are lined up in a row and moved through narrow runways leading to a chute with spring-loaded gates. When a calf enters the chute, the gate is closed behind it and a lightweight 28-foot rope, attached to a trip lever, is fastened around the calf's neck. The lever holds a taut cord or "barrier" that runs across a large pen or "box" at one side of the calf chute where the horse and rider wait.

The barrier is used to ensure that the calf gets a head start. When the roper is ready, he calls for the calf, and the chute operator pulls a lever opening the chute doors and releases the calf. The calf runs in a straight line. When the calf reaches the end of the rope, that trips a lever and the rope falls off the calf. The barrier for the horse and rider is released, starting the clock and allowing horse and rider to chase the calf.

Timing is very important for winning the contest. From a standstill, James must spur his horse into a full gallop to chase the calf. Therefore, the burst of the horse out of the chute is very important.

James then would lasso the calf from horseback by throwing a loop of the lariat around the calf's neck. Once the rope is around the calf's neck, James quickly dismounts and runs to the calf.

The calf must be stopped by the rope. If the calf falls, James would need to allow the calf to get back on its feet. When James reaches the calf, he picks it up and flips it onto its side. Once the calf is on the ground, James ties three of the calf's legs together with a short rope known as a tie-down rope or "piggin' string."

James always carried his piggin' string in his teeth to save time until he was ready to tie the legs of the calf. After the tie, James would throw up his hands to signal "time" and stop the clock.

James would then return to his horse, mount and move the horse forward to relax the tension on the rope. The timer waits for six seconds, during which the calf must stay tied before an official time is recorded. James would usually tie a calf in from 8 to 9 seconds. Later, a cowboy in Cheyenne, Wyoming's Frontier Days set the world record of just over 6 seconds.

It was on Sunday, December 7th of 1941 that after having their large dinner the men had gathered around the radio to listen to the Sunday afternoon football game.

The Author

Chapter 24

World War II

On Sundays many families would attend a church closest to where they lived. Stella and Eric now owned a mansion in Belle Fourche, while Marion and Charlene resided on a ranch just outside Belle Fourche.

After attending one of the protestant churches, the individual families would gather between noon and 1 P.M. for a large dinner.

It was on Sunday, December 7th of 1941 that after having their large dinner, the men gathered around the radio to listen to the Sunday afternoon football game between the Chicago Bears and the Chicago Cardinals. Overheard on the radio was the public address announcer telling all military servicemen to report to their posts.

The men listened more intently for further details. There was really no other "breaking news" to report, so as they were in the fourth quarter, the game continued until completion with the Bears winning the game thirty-four to twenty-four.

Later on the radio announcer gave the startling report that the Japanese had bombed Pearl Harbor.

All the families in the area were very concerned as they suspected that their sons would be needed to either join one of the armed services or wait to be drafted.

During these difficult times many of the sons were excluded from the draft as they would be needed to raise crops or livestock to support the armed services and the United States allies.

Many of the boys in the area thought it their patriotic duty to join immediately. Cooler heads prevailed, and most of the families in the area agreed that the oldest son should stay on the farm or ranch, while the younger boys who were at least 18 years old would join one of the branches of the armed services.

There were exceptions to having the oldest boy stay at home. Both David and James received the permission of their parents to join one of the branches of the military.

Button's boy John had already served in the military, so he was too old to be drafted. Sarah's other boy Harry was also beyond draft age since he was just a couple of years younger than John.

Therefore, the very next Monday, December 8th, the parents of both David and James drove into Rapid City so that the boys could join the military.

David, being the more adventures of the two boys joined the marines, while James would join the navy.

The two boys were given one week before each was to report to his training station.

However, both boys wanted a last "fling" in Deadwood as a way of saying goodbye to civilian life.

David did not tell his parents that he had "broken up" with his girlfriend Sue Ann about a month before. Therefore, the boys wanted real adventure and attempted to enter the Gem Theater in Deadwood.

After climbing the stairs to the Gem Theater's second floor rooms, they knocked on the outside door. The madam opened the peep hole in the door and then opened the door to tell the boys they were too young to participate in the activities that were taking place in the many private rooms.

David, being the bolder of the two, asked why they couldn't just look at the girls in their very skimpy costumes before leaving.

The madam quickly slammed the door shut. The boys were upset, as they had saved a few bucks working on the ranch to pay for their entertainment. The boys took the stairs down and left the Gem. They found a bar that would serve them a beer. However, even the bartender would serve only one beer each.

Next, as it was too early to head back to the ranch, they decided to get a good steak at the Franklin Hotel. At least there was one activity where they could receive service.

After finishing the steak, the boys sat on the grand porch of the hotel and watched the people pass by. Many a cowboy entered and later left the Gem. David said to his cousin James, "Damn madam, we look as old as the cowboys passing on the street."

James noticed an old prospector handing out autographs to a few of the people on the porch. James asked his cousin, "Who is that old fellow and why are all the people interested in him?"

David answered, "Why, don't you recognize Potato Creek Johnnie?" James was always the curious one and wanted to know more of the story, and so he motioned Mr. Perret over to where they were sitting.

Johnnie stood only a little over four feet tall with a white beard that grew down to almost touching his belt buckle. The old prospector also wore a dirty hat that was a bit too large for him. It appeared that his blue jeans had not been washed for at least a year.

With encouragement from the boys, Johnnie pulled up a rocking chair and proceeded to tell them the story of the largest gold nugget found in the Black Hills.

Johnnie first told them, "I want you boys to know that my nugget was panned on the Potato Creek – not the Spearfish Creek as many authorities will tell you."

"Second, is the vicious rumor that I stole a few gold pieces from my neighbors and melted them together to form my nine ounce nugget is totally false."

When David asked what happened to the nugget, Johnnie told them that he had sold the piece to Mr. W.E. Adams for the grand total of $250 in 1929. Johnnie went on to say that he should have waited to sell the nugget as the price of gold was much higher today.

Johnnie said that Mr. Adams had placed a replica of the nugget in his museum for people to see, and that the real nugget was placed in the museum safe.

After a few minutes of silence as the boys pondered the story, Johnnie told them it was getting late and he thought he should ride back to his cabin for the night.

In parting Johnnie told the boys that they would be welcome to visit him as he still panned for more gold on the Potato Creek.

It was while James was on board his ship that he read in the *Stars and Stripes* newspaper that Potato Creek Johnny had died in February of 1943.

The newspaper article further elaborated that when the funeral procession passed by the Adams Museum the carillon chimes tolled 77 times – the age of Mr. Perret when he died.

"Potato Creek" had the honor of being buried next to Wild Bill Hickok and Calamity Jane in the Mt. Moriah Cemetery.

"Well, private, then you have just received your assignment for the next invasion. I want you on a very secret mission."

Major General Clayton B. Vogel

Chapter 25

David is Now a Marine

David reported to Paris Island, South Carolina. On the first day, recruit Anderson was told to perform twenty push-ups for the group. Being a strong young man David had no difficulty with this order. However, he did need to hold his temper when the sergeant was spitting on him as he gave additional orders that to David were just damn stupid.

The young men were assigned bunks in the two-story wooden barracks, and then jogged to another portion of the base to have their heads shaved. Next they received the clothes they would be wearing while in the marines.

The enlisted men shoving clothes at the recruits were not too careful in getting the sizes correct, and so many of the young men's caps or pants were either too big or too small.

Luckily, David's boots fit perfectly and this would end up being the most important aspect of the Marine attire, as immediately they would be running everywhere on base. After dressing in their uniforms, they were issued the standard M-1 rifle.

Weeks passed as they marched, completed calisthenics, learned to fire their weapons, clean their weapons and take apart and put together their M-1s.

During the second eight weeks, the recruits were introduced to other weapons they would be using in the coming battles.

When the basic training and advanced weapons training were completed, the men participated in a graduation ceremony before being assigned to various fighting units.

David was assigned to an infantry unit bound for the South Pacific. After taking a train across the entire United States the group boarded troop ships to take them to Hawaii.

One morning David was approached by a young corporal and told to immediately report to the base headquarters.

David jogged to the headquarters thinking that perhaps something had happened to his family back in South Dakota.

Instead, Private Anderson was ushered into Major General Clayton B. Vogel's office. General Vogel was the commanding general of the Amphibious Corps for the entire Pacific Fleet.

After properly saluting the General, Private Anderson was ordered to stand at parade rest. The General asked Private Anderson if he had grown up with any Indians. David responded, "Yes sir, there were a number of both Sioux and Cheyenne Indians in South Dakota."

The General then responded with the words, "Then private you do not harbor any ill feelings in having Indians serving in the war?"

Private Anderson immediately stated, "No Sir, some of my best friends were Indian."

"Well private, then you have just received your assignment for the next invasion. I want you on a very secret mission."

As it turned out David was assigned to protect a Navajo Code Talker. The captain on the invasion fleet ordered David to protect his assigned Navajo with his life. David was told that if there were any chance of the two of them being captured, then David was to kill the Navajo.

At first David did not understand the order. Then he realized that a skilled Japanese interrogator would torture the Indian and thus learn the language of the Code Talkers. This order was a bit much for David to swallow as he became very close friends with Sgt. John Danforth, the Navajo assigned to him.

With the new assignment David was promoted to corporal. It took a while for David to sew on his new stripes, but he was proud of this promotion and his new friend Sgt. Danforth.

While being transported on a naval vessel to the unit's invasion station near Iwo Jima the two men had time to talk on the fan tail of the troop ship.

David was very curious and wanted to know more about John and his knowledge of the Navajo language. John explained that his native language was not even a written language. Also, this language was spoken only on his homeland in northwest Arizona.

As John had studied one year at Arizona State University, he was able to further tell David that the syntax and tonal qualities, not to mention dialects, made it unintelligible to anyone without extensive exposure and training.

Sgt. Danforth was studying his native language when he was drafted. At Arizona State Sgt. Danforth was told by a professor that in about 1940, fewer than 30 non-Navajos could understand the language.

Sgt. Danforth pulled from his jacket pocket a codebook that was developed to teach the many relevant words and concepts to both new and veteran Code Talkers. John explained to David that this codebook was not to be taken onto the island when they landed.

John often excused himself in the evenings. He explained that he needed to study the codebook to memorize all the variations and to practice the rapid use under stressful conditions. Those natives on the receiving end of the messages would hear only truncated and disjointed strings of individual, unrelated nouns and verbs.

Due to the value of the Code Talkers, they would not be among the first wave of marines to land on the beaches. Instead, it was about the third group of marines where John and David found themselves churning toward the enemy land. There were still water spouts as enemy shells tried to hit the landing barges.

Major Howard Connor of the 5th Marine Division was serving as the signal officer. The Major had only six Navajo Code Talkers assigned to his division. Of course, each Code Talker was accompanied by a trained marine for protection.

It was reported that over 800 messages were given and received without a single error. Major Connor was reported to have later stated, "Were it not for the Navajos, the marines would never have taken Iwo Jima."

However, there were mass causalities among the invading marines. None of the Navajos was killed, but unfortunately, David was in a fierce firefight when a Japanese soldier threw a grenade into the foxhole where the two men were hunkered down.

Immediately, David threw himself on top of Sgt. Danforth saving his life. David was very seriously wounded and had to be taken aboard a hospital ship to treat his injuries. The corpsmen on board the ship did not expect David to live through the night.

When the hospital ship docked in Hawaii, it was none other than General Clayton Vogel who walked into the medical ward and pinned both a Purple Heart and a Bronze Star on David's top sheet.

David was in terrible pain and so the nurses kept him sedated for several days. In the middle of the night in the second week, David screamed at the top of his lungs when he looked down at his bed sheet and viewed only one leg. The doctors on board the hospital ship had to remove his right leg just above the knee.

After crying himself to sleep, the next morning all David could think about was that his days of participating in rodeos in his home state were over. Severe depression took over and the medical staff thought that after spending some time in San Francisco, he should be transferred to Fort Meade, South Dakota, to be closer to his family.

During the later years of the war, Fort Meade was primarily a veterans' hospital as the cavalry was now all mechanized.

Chapter 26

James Joins the Navy

As soon as James arrived in San Diego, the bus taking the young men to the base stopped and a navy chief stepped aboard to welcome his young recruits.

Perhaps the greeting was somewhat more pleasant than what David experienced when he was met by his marine sergeant. However, the chief soon let the young men know who exactly was in charge.

The new recruits received the standard buzz cut with the long locks of hair piling up under the barber's chair.

Next the men jogged to another building to be fitted with the standard navy uniforms. Next they marched to the two-story wooden barracks where they quickly found their bunks. Some disagreements broke out on who would occupy the upper bunk.

The chief ended his lecture with the statement that when you find yourself on board a ship you will be swinging in a hammock. One of the young men from Chicago then "smarted off" and stated that this sounded like a vacation on board a ship.

Well, this was a big mistake as the smart-aleck was first cussed out by the chief before being taken outside and made to run a couple of miles around the barracks. This would teach a lesson to the other men under the chief's command.

Very early the next morning the recruits were awakened before dawn to take care of any bathroom duties including a close shave. Then they made their beds so tight that a quarter would bounce off the top blanket.

After formation the men marched to the mess hall for their morning chow before jogging to a building for a battery of tests. The tests would determine which of the new recruits had the intelligence to proceed with further schooling and which recruits would immediately move on to the standard boot training. Of course, having high scores on the mental tests would not exempt the men from performing calisthenics and being yelled at by the cadre.

The advanced schooling for those having high scores would have to wait until all the recruits passed the basic portion of their training.

The two most important aspects of naval training were to be able to survive in the water and to deal with a fire on board a ship. Therefore, a majority of the recruits' time was spent on these two aspects of training. At least a week was spent on being familiar with small arms such as a rifle and a pistol – but not to the extent that was emphasized by the Army and Marines.

James' scores were not quite high enough for him to have more advanced schooling. Therefore, he would be placed in the engine room of an assigned ship after completion of the basic training.

James really didn't like to be confined in the hole of a ship as he had been raised on the open plains of South Dakota. He so hoped to land duty topside so he could smell the salt air.

Being around farm implements most of his life gave James a "leg up" on understanding the mechanics of the engine room. The boys who grew up in the cities had a much tougher time in learning their assigned duties.

It didn't take long for this recruiting class to complete their training and participate in the graduation parade. As it was a long drive from South Dakota to California none of the family witnessed James' graduation. Because of the war there was now imposed rationing on gasoline and other items such as tires.

Eventually after chow at noon one day an announcement was made over the intercom that the postings had been listed on the bulletin boards outside each mess hall.

Anxious to find out what type of ship they would be assigned, the young men didn't finish their meals. Instead, they ran outside to find their postings.

Of course, some of the recruits were happy – but not James. James found that he would be assigned to the engine room of a destroyer. The lucky ones would be placed on a larger ship such as a battleship or carrier. The bigger ships could plow through the rough seas without all the men getting seasick. The carriers and battleships also had more space and more recreational facilities.

It was imperative that the United States Navy quickly assemble a fleet to stop the Japanese expansion in the South Pacific. Therefore, a fleet of ships under the command of William (Bull) Halsey made due haste to its assigned location.

Seaman Hall was assigned to the destroyer *USS Tabberer* – a small *John C. Butler*-class destroyer escort. This small destroyer escort was part of the much larger Third Fleet that was operating east of Luzon in the Philippine Sea.

The *USS Tabberer* was part of TF 38 consisting of seven fleet carriers, six light carriers, eight battleships, 15 cruisers and about 50 destroyers. The carriers had been conducting raids against Japanese airfields in the Philippines.

Bad weather struck the fleet just a few days after leaving harbor. Although there might have been some warning of an approaching typhoon, Admiral Halsey thought the storm would not be dangerous enough to stop the continued bombing of the airfields on the Japanese islands.

As the smaller destroyers did not carry as much fuel, the *USS Tabberer* was attempting to be refueled when the typhoon hit the area. Quickly, the refueling was aborted.

A few ships experienced rolls of over 70 percent and damage suffered by the fleet was severe. Three destroyers, *Spence*, *Hickox* and *Maddox* had nearly empty fuel stores and therefore lacked the stabilizing effect of the extra weight and thus were relatively unstable.

Additionally, several other of the older *Farragut*-class had been refitted with over 500 long tons of extra equipment and armament which made them top-heavy.

The destroyers *Spence*, *Hull* and *Monaghan* were sunk either by capsizing outright, or as a result of water down-flooding through their smokestacks and disabling their engines. Without power, they were unable to control their heading and were at the mercy of the wind and seas.

Hickox and *Maddox*, due to ballasting of their empty fuel tanks, had greater stability and were able to ride out the storm with relatively minor damage. Probably, survival was due to the bright thinking of the captain of each of these destroyers who had pumped seawater into the fuel tanks to make them more stable.

The *USS Tabberer* lost her mast and radio antennas. Though the ship was damaged and unable to radio for help, the captain took the initiative to remain on the scene to recover 55 of the 93 total men who were rescued.

But in the hole of the *Tabberer* where James was working, the ship's rolling had thrown him into a metal pipe and knocked him unconscious. At first the medics on board thought Seaman James would recover fine, but he failed to gain consciousness and at the first opportunity they transferred him to a hospital ship.

The hospital ship, with full capacity, made its way to San Francisco and James remained in a hospital for over a month. His parents, Marion and Charlene were able to borrow enough gasoline stamps and purchase new tires with the help of the good citizens of Faith, Belle Fourche and surrounding communities to make the drive to San Francisco.

A navy surgeon met the family in the waiting room and told them the sad news that although a risky surgery was required, James would need a steel plate placed in his head, just above his left ear. The blow to his head had seriously damaged his skull.

The surgery was successful and after another month in the hospital, followed with six additional weeks of physical therapy, James was able to be transferred to the hospital at Fort Meade, South Dakota.

Chapter 27

Cole is Drafted by the Army

Marion and Charlene's youngest son Cole waited to be drafted by the army as he thought that he would be needed on the ranch. However, in early 1945, Cole received his official letter to report to Fort Leonard Wood for basic training.

Very similar to what David and James had experienced, Cole was met by a very big and tough sergeant who would soon have the drafted recruits into combat ready soldiers.

Unlike David and James who experienced combat in the Pacific Theatre, Cole survived both basic and advanced infantry training and was soon on a troop ship to Europe.

The war was winding down and Cole was indeed fortunate as he was assigned to guarding German soldiers as they were brought back from the front lines.

It was somewhat of a weird situation that many German soldiers were shipped to Belle Fourche, South Dakota. A prison had been constructed and the captured Germans were put to work harvesting sugar beets and performing other menial tasks.

While in France Cole met and would fall in love with a French girl by the name of Monique. Soon the two were married in Paris by the army chaplain.

The red-tape was very frustrating to the young couple as it appeared that it would probably take months for Monique to make the passage to the United States.

The first priority was to bring the G.I.s home and then to bring the wives and in some cases their children. Monique and Cole did not have children, and both decided they would wait until they were united in the States to think about a family.

Many evenings were spent with Cole telling his wife about his brother James and his cousin David. He had received news about their horrific injuries and their transfer to Fort Meade, South Dakota.

As Monique understood English quite well, she wanted Cole to tell all about life in the United States and in particular about his family. During these long evening conversations Cole told Monique about how both David and James had participated in rodeos.

Cole described how Uncle Roy Hall had taught Button's boys and himself how to use a lariat and impress everyone who watched. By trial and error Cole had learned the tricks of using the lariat and swirling the rope in ever larger circles.

Cole said that being a very good horseback rider, he would also swirl his lariat while riding his trusty stead. He had even perfected the daring stunt of standing on his saddle and swirled the rope. To even complicate the stunt the horse would be galloping by the grandstand.

Monique was fascinated with these stories. She knew nothing about living on a ranch, nor had she ever heard of lariats or rodeos.

Cole's parents thought that his stunts were a much safer way to perform at rodeos than what David and James were doing in the rodeos.

As soon as Cole was able to return to the States, he received an Honorable Discharge in New York.

Hopping a bus, Cole rode a couple of days and nights to South Dakota. After greeting his entire family, he took the family pick-up to Fort Meade to visit David and James.

During Cole's absence his parents had raised two beautiful Collie dogs – one female by the name of Lassie and a male by the name of Prince.

Cole encouraged Prince and Lassie to jump into the back of the pickup to drive from the ranch to the hospital at Fort Meade. It seems that all dogs love to ride in a car or truck. Cole thought that the two dogs would encourage David and James in their recovery.

At first the head nurse was not going to allow the dogs in the hospital. However, the head doctor by the name of Larson ordered the nurse to attend to her other duties and the doctor – a full colonel – led Cole and the two dogs down the polished wooden floor of the hospital.

Both James and David were in the same ward and were greatly surprised to see Cole. Immediately, the two dogs ran to one bed and then the other and put their paws and heads on the boy's bed.

So to receive equal attention, Cole encouraged Lassie to jump on David's bed and Prince to jump on James's bed. With this move the colonel, with tears in his eyes, departed the ward.

Doctor Larson had seen too much of the war casualties, and he thought that he just couldn't stand much more of seeing such promising young men returning from the war to end up in such bad situations.

When Cole asked the patients how they were doing, both grinned from ear to ear. Both had established a very good relationship with a couple of beautiful nurses.

To make a long story short the two nurses, Arlene and Jean had accepted the boys' proposals for marriage. The plans were for the four of them to have a joint wedding in the beautiful meadow called "Blue Belle" near Hot Springs, South Dakota.

The Blue Belle is a very pretty wild flower that blooms in early spring among the meadows of the southern Black Hills, near Hot Springs. As the flower reaches its full bloom in April, the plans were made to have the wedding at this time.

As soon as the cousins were well enough to be released from the hospital, the wedding took place. For their honeymoon the four spent a week at a very nice hotel in Hot Springs, South Dakota. The warm mineral water was very soothing to the war wounds of both David and James.

It should be noted that the wounds suffered by the young men did not affect their ability to have children.

However, with increasing technology, the operation of equipment needed to be changed from horses to gasoline-operated tractors and trucks.

The Author

Chapter 28

Uncle Roy and Button's Family

Both of Button's boys John and Harry married local girls and moved to Greeley, Colorado. Stella and Eric had the need for management personnel to oversee their ever increasing business operations in Colorado.

The business operation consisted of establishing feed lots to prepare cattle for shipment to markets in Omaha and Chicago. The business expanded and profited and soon John and Harry had exceeded even the wildest dreams of Stella and Eric.

Meanwhile, Roy and Button's youngest son, Everett, would stay on the homestead just outside Faith, South Dakota, and eventually take over the operation of the ranch.

This was a very healthy arrangement as Uncle Roy and Button were now approaching that age when the manual labor needed to operate a large cattle ranch was taxing, even for younger men.

The summers on the plains continued to be hot and dry and the winters harsh. However, the ever increasing technology available made the operation of large ranches much easier. Gasoline operated trucks and tractors replaced the horse-drawn wagons.

Also, the living standards improved considerably. Now the ranchers had indoor plumbing, running water and electricity. Also, highway 212 now ran very close to the Hall ranch. At first the highway was gravel and mud, but eventually the United States Government paved the major highway that joined the eastern part of the state to the west and beyond.

Uncle Roy, Button and Everett built a very fine home that all would share. The home was large enough that Everett had his own living quarters. Unlike, his two older brothers and cousins, Everett liked the life of living as a bachelor and would never marry.

Everett did have a social life and was well liked by all the neighbors. He often socialized in Faith by attending such events as the Fourth of July celebration, Christmas parties and private parties. It was reported that Everett dated a widow lady living in Newell, South Dakota. In fact, the two of them attended many social gatherings together.

Everett's very attractive friend Elizabeth was reported to have been widowed at a very young age and could never bring herself to form a loving relationship with another man.

Elizabeth worked in the only bank in Newell and with the assistance from an insurance policy left by her dearly departed husband maintained a lovely little house only one block from the main street of Newell.

A few "nosey" neighbors reported that Everett would be seen leaving Elizabeth's home early on Monday mornings after spending the weekend in Newell.

Prior to most of the guests having arrived, Cole Hall with wife Monique had purposely been early to sample the imported French champagne and make sure all of the arrangements were in order.

The Author

Chapter 29

Conclusion

It seemed as if the entire populations of both Belle Fourche and Spearfish were assembled in the Crystal Room of the Bullock Hotel in Belle Fourche when all of the Halls and Andersons made their grand entrance. A huge crystal chandelier sparkled above the throng of elegantly dressed citizens.

The men looked splendid in their pressed tuxedos; the women were elegant in their evening gowns with jewels. A few of the wranglers from nearby ranches wore their best dress-up cowboy boots with either their best blue suits or tuxedos. Nevertheless, the boots were all polished so that one could see that the men had spent considerable time in preparing for this special event.

There was a feeling of festivity in the air as the gathering mingled and sipped the very best champagne imported from France. A few of the wranglers tried the caviar, but the waiters did notice that very few would help themselves to a second serving.

Virginia and Frank Hall entered the ballroom holding hands. It was evident to the rest of the assembled crowd that they were very proud of their children and grandchildren. Both seemed in good health and wore genuine smiles on their faces.

Stella Hall Anderson, wearing a gown of bright blue chiffon and nearly all of the jewels that her husband had given her over the past several years, slowly moved around the grand ballroom, speaking to just about everyone. Her husband Eric pushed Uncle Roy Hall's wheelchair among the assembled guests speaking in his customary loud voice to friends, neighbors and business acquaintances. With Roy's crippling arthritis it was difficult for him to walk. Button walked proudly beside her husband.

The Anderson's son David with his wife Arlene moved among the guests shaking hands and receiving pats on the back. He still appreciated the many words of thanks he received for the sacrifice of losing his right leg in the war. David was still using his crutches that evening; therefore, he held tight to the arm of his beautiful wife.

Marion, Charlene, James and Jean arrived a little later. It was sometimes difficult for James to gather the nerve to meet so many people. James was still having adjustment problems after leaving Fort Meade's medical center. The ever-smiling and gorgeous Jean caught the eye of every man in the ballroom as she strode through the crowd in her brightly colored red ballroom dress. It seemed that even with the problems that James was undergoing, she still looked very happy.

Prior to most of the guests having arrived, Cole Hall with wife Monique had purposefully been early to sample the champagne and make sure all of the arrangements were in order.

Both sons of Sarah Cummings Hall, John and Harry, along with their wives, were seen coming in one of the side doors of the grand hotel. Even Everett and best friend Elizabeth were sighted among the guests.

The last to arrive was Tex Bennett and wife Maria. Casey Bennett came with his parents and was immediately drawn to the punch bowl of champagne. The younger Bennett boy Leslie had taken a job in another state and did not attend.

Only Eleanor, daughter of Marion and Charlene, was missing from the gathering. She was suffering from a very severe cold, and Dr. Dawson advised that she not attend. Since he was her husband, he stayed home to care for her.

The celebration was to honor the generous gift that Eric and Stella Anderson and Frank and Virginia Hall had given the city of Belle Fourche. It seemed that enough money was generated to build a modern new high school. The school was to be furnished with the very best of anything money could buy. Even Bedford stone from central Indiana was hauled by train to form the outside of the school.

Stella spotted Uncle Roy from across the room and glided to where he was sitting, came to a standstill next to him and planted a kiss on his forehead.

"What an occasion this is," Roy said, beaming. "Finally a legacy is being given to the town that has been so good to all of us."

Always the emotional one in the family, Cole was heard to say to his wife Monique, "I wish that our grandparents could be here to witness this grand occasion."

Overhearing this statement, it was Marion who said in a loud enough voice that nearly everyone would hear, "Yes indeed, but you know they are smiling down upon us from their Heavenly place above."

As the mayor and superintendent stood together on the stage, Mayor Stillwater gave a toast to the Anderson and Hall families. Mayor Stillwater said in a loud and clear voice, "Let us all raise our glasses to the wonderful families who have brought this town together and so generously shared in their great wealth." A picture of the planned building was unveiled for everyone to admire.

The evening wore on with the orchestra playing waltz music so that the guests could enjoy the evening. It should be noted that most of the wranglers stood around the edge of the ballroom sipping their drinks of whiskey that they bought from the hotel bar. It seemed as if the best champagne – even though it came from Paris – just didn't settle with them.

When James asked Cole how Prince and Lassie were doing, it was Monique who laughed and said, "Haven't you heard, the two of them are taking care of their just born family of six little pups."

"Oh yes," said Cole "The Hall Dynasty must continue."

Epilogue

As author of the book *FROM DESPAIR TO FORTUNE* I have had personal knowledge of two of the real-life characters.

I am now in my late 70's and as a young boy of about ten or twelve my father, an ATF Agent, took me with him to Deadwood, South Dakota. While we were sitting in rocking chairs on the grand porch of the Franklin Hotel, Potato Creek Johnnie came to talk with my father.

The two were acquainted as my father, Charles E. Campbell, had been to Deadwood many times to check the Federal Liquor Licenses of the many bars in town. Johnnie jointed us on the porch and I listened with awe to Johnnie's tales of panning for gold.

The second character that I actually knew about is Poker Alice. Although I never met the "lady," my father arrested her for the manufacture and distribution of moonshine. It seemed that in addition to playing poker, selling legal or taxed liquor, and being the madam of the brothel, she was also selling the liquor she had made in the back of her establishment.

I grew up in Rapid City, South Dakota, and our home was just below "Hangman's Hill." As a boy I climbed the hill, along with my buddies, and together we would shoot our BB guns. At the time the pine tree, although dead, was still being supported by sealed rock around the base of the tree.

If you are a tourist in Rapid City it is possible to ride a trolley from the Holiday Inn located along Rapid Creek to explore the historical sites of the city. On the tour the trolley will take tourists on a winding road to the top of "Hangman's Hill" to view the location of where the hanging of James Hall took place in the 1800's. The trolley will run only in the summer months, due to the sometimes harsh winters experienced in western South Dakota.

I also remember the snow blizzard occurring in 1949, when cargo planes from Ellsworth Air Base dropped bales of hay to the cattle in northwest South Dakota. The snow drifts were so high that the ranchers could not get feed to the cattle.

While in Rapid City, tourists can visit the Indian Museum located within a block of the Holiday Inn where they can catch the trolley. At the museum visitors can see authentic Indian artifacts.

I graduated from Rapid City Central High School in 1954 and have been back for several of my class reunions. The city has changed, but not so much as to distract from my memories.

As far as Deadwood, South Dakota, is concerned tourists will still find gambling and other vices that the "city fathers" allow. In the summer the Chamber of Commerce features a "running gun battle" down the streets of the city. The festivities end with a trial of Jack McCall. He is the cowboy who shot Wild Bill Hickok in the back in Saloon Number 10.

Also, the "Days of 76" rodeo is still held in August. If you schedule a tour to travel to the Black Hills, I encourage you to take in this very entertaining event.

Printed in the USA
CPSIA information can be obtained
at www.ICGtesting.com
CBHW071101190424
7118CB00009B/157

9 781608 624942